MISSING ON LION ROCK

PATRICIA SNELLING

Published in New Zealand by Patricia Snelling

Contact: patricia.snelling.books@gmail.com
Website: patriciasnelling.com

Copyright Patricia Snelling 2020

This is a work of fiction. Any resemblance to actual persons, living or dead, or actual events is purely coincidental and not to be construed as real.

A catalogue record for this book is available from the National Library of New Zealand

Harold Joyce Cover Art - Martin Joyce Graphic Design
Editing Support – Judith Little

****

Other Books by Author:

When Hope Went South (Dart River #1)
Jessie's High Country Heart (Dart River #2)
Mack The Good Shepherd (Dart River #3)
Missing On Kawau
Unshakable
Broken Web
Rescue Net
Louis's Garden Party (Preschooler's book)

****

Website: patriciasnelling.com

Chapter One

Sandy Barrett struggled up the last few metres of the overgrown dirt track to the lookout which was steep enough to suck the breath from her lungs—a reminder of how long it had been since her last bush walk.

At the summit she perched on the stone bench at the side of the track to catch her breath, staring into the abyss of the ocean before her, which matched the intense blue of the spring sky.

A strange sound caught her attention. Was the bizarre sound the cry of a child or an animal? The screech of a creature in pain sent chilling ripples up her spine. She got to her feet and looked around. Her heart somersaulted as she saw movement in the tussock grass at the side of the track.

Edging her way towards the edge of the cliff, she shuddered at the thought of slipping down the hundred-foot drop to the rocks below.

Her face fell at the pitiful sight of a great, black-backed gull trapped in a tree branch, its legs bound by fishing line. The hideous squawking made her blood curl.

Aware of the friable clay holding the edge of the bank together, she trod warily towards the frightened animal.

'It's okay, baby, I'll help you. Shush, keep calm and I'll be there.'

To Sandy's relief, her voice seemed to soothe the bird.

Grateful she was wearing shoes with tractor soles, she eased her way towards the branch that had taken the bird hostage. To her horror, it protruded over a sheer precipice with rocks below.

She remembered the penknife she kept in her day pack and knew that one day she would find a use for it. Sharp twigs spiked her legs as she crept with trepidation towards the worn-out bird. Reaching for the branch, she held onto it with one hand while cutting the nylon from its legs as it struggled and flailed at the same time.

In an instant, realising it was free the bird escaped, its large wings whipping her face and blinding her as the creature ascended into oblivion. After closing the penknife and putting it back into her pocket, she turned around to return to the walking track when suddenly her feet lost their grip. Her body jettisoned like batman off the cliff face, sharp branches smacking her in the face on the way down. She screamed as a large tree branch broke her fall. Her ribs felt like they'd shattered into tiny pieces, and then she passed out. Her lifeless body lay on a rocky ledge several metres high above the seashore below. Unconsciousness seized her.

🐾 🐾 🐾

At 8 am the sun raised its cheery face to greet Sandy's close friends, Peter Epston and Elly Brownley, as the two buddies wound up their daily meditation and chat on Lion Rock—this time, without Sandy. It had been an early morning ritual for the three friends, and their special way of starting the day. Rarely did any of them miss it.

But this morning was different as they were perplexed that neither of them had received a text message from Sandy when she had failed to appear. They finished their fellowship time together—eager to get over to her flat to find out what had happened.

They traipsed up the dune next to her house just in time to catch Briar, Sandy's flatmate before she shot off to the rest home where she worked as a nurse.

She scraped meat from a can into the dog's bowl. 'Hi, you two—what are you doing here and where's Sandy? You usually go over to your house for coffee after your morning meetings before work, don't you, Elly?'

'We do—but Sandy didn't turn up. We didn't even get a message from her, which is quite out of character.' Elly checked her text messages again.

'I hope she's alright—I have to get to work sorry. She probably had to run an errand and forgot to let you know. She'd slept in her bed last night, but I didn't wake until after she'd left the house early this morning. She left a note to ask if I would feed Sleuth, as she was leaving the house early to go off somewhere.'

'I've got your number so I'll text you if I hear anything,' said Elly.

'And I'll do the same,' replied Briar.

Chapter Two

There was far too much at stake for Carlos to lose this far down track. The 10 kg of cocaine was worth millions of dollars and the luxury New Zealand yacht that hid the stash was a perfect example of the kind of wealth possible from supplying class A drugs at $360 per gram. A mothership had transported illicit cargo from Colombia through the South Pacific to Sydney, where it had been transferred to the yacht's hull.

Carlos and his crew met the yacht in the Far North that had come from the Bay of Islands. They drew close to the yacht in their powerful cabin boat, under the guise of local fishermen, and moored onto a buoy. On the deck sat crates of fresh fish on ice, just to baffle the Coast Guard if they were stopped.

'Let's get going before the sun goes down. It'll be pretty murky down there,' Carlos said brusquely, as Kingi Walker donned his wet suit in the cabin. His side-kick, Manuel Santos, scanned the waters, making sure they had not been spotted.

Kingi looked around and then ventured down the ladder into the water and swam to the yacht to fetch the bag of drugs hidden behind the rudder. He was Carlos's prize diver and worked quickly.

Kingi and Manuel had been well-drilled by Carlos about what to do if they were caught. The packets were wrapped in watertight packing, stuffed inside a waterproof duffel bag so that they could dump them overboard if necessary.

Kingi landed the bag onto the deck of the fishing boat. 'There you are—10 kg of white gold. No time to count them—let's clear out of here.'

Carlos worked swiftly, attaching a weight to the bag. If they had to offload it in a hurry, external divers waited on standby onshore, ready to retrieve the bag when it was safe.

'Just keep your eyes peeled and your ears open for the faintest sign of an approaching vessel and the bag goes overboard,' snarled Carlos.

The fishing boat belonged to one of Carlos's employees who dropped them off at a remote beach on the West Coast. There they transferred the precious cargo to his own speedy amphibious rib boat that one of his cartel's men left waiting for them. This boat would take them back to his vehicle parked in Woodhill Forest near the shores of Muriwai Beach—but first Carlos would need to drop Manuel off as his bach at Whites Beach further along the coast.

'Not long to go now till the end of a darn good day's work. Thanks, you guys—here, crack open a beer if you want, but keep your eye out for any sign of life,' said Carlos, his mood relaxing a little as he revved up the engine and sped off towards Whites Beach.

The men grabbed a bottle of beer each that Carlos had stored in the cooler early that morning. Kingi tried to relax, but he seemed agitated. 'Are you okay mate?' Manuel asked his friend.

'Yeah, just knocked the stuffing out of me a bit this time. Getting too old for this game now, I guess.'

Carlos swung around from the helm and glared at him.

'Why don't you just sit down? You're winding me up,' he snapped.

Manuel looked across at Kingi who caught sight of him in the moonlight rolling his eyes at Carlos who few people dared to cross. He controlled his followers by fear, but this time Kingi's tolerance was wearing thin. He learnt enough during his drug rehab to know he had choices and didn't have to be controlled by substances or by other people. This time he had succumbed to temptation, but he didn't think he could go through it again. He resented Carlos who had threatened he would harm his family if he refused to participate in this major cocaine haul. He said he owed him, which was a lie, but because of their history, he did not refute it.

Kingi had let his mother and the whanau down. When he went into rehab the last time, he promised his mother he would stay clean and go straight, and now this will break her heart. A sharp twinge of pain caused by the guilt rippled through his neck. He had failed her and himself—but no more.

Chapter Three

Friday

Sandy covered her face with her hands as she woke, shielding herself from the late afternoon sun scorching her head. The fair skin on her face stung as she wrinkled up her eyes.

Desperate words tumbled from her bruised mouth as she regained consciousness, recalling every minute of the horror that had gone before. 'God help me—please!' *How long have I been out cold? By the position of the sun, it must have been hours.*

She let out a muted groan as she tried to inhale. 'Ahhh!' *My ribs must be shattered. Where am I?*

She had a clear recollection of rescuing a bird and losing her footing. Glancing upwards, she saw that she must have fallen at least fifty metres if it hadn't been for a robust branch breaking her fall. If not for this saving grace, she'd have tumbled another fifty metres to her death.

You'd better think fast or prepare for a long night ahead.

She had to work out a way to attract attention, but no one would hear her on the beach below or the track above in such dense bush. Excruciating pain sickened her as she dragged her battered body like an injured dog aside from the tea tree that blocked her view. She stiffened, aghast as she identified her location from the rocky ledge overlooking Whites Beach.

Although she was grateful her day pack had stayed on during the fall, she was upset she'd lost her hat. 'Help me, someone—please help me!' she called, repeating her plea a few times before she wilted. She had to get out of the unrelenting heat. *How is anyone going to hear me from here? That's what you get for your obsession with bird rescue!*

'Oh, no—I'm doomed,' she murmured as she crawled away from the rocky ledge.

Were her eyes playing tricks on her like a mirage? She could see a rocky cave in the side of the cliff face where she could shelter from the elements.

With all the strength she could muster, she dragged herself into the shade of the cave and passed out again. When she came to, she started jabbering out loud, either to talk to her creator or to find comfort in talking to herself. No answer, just the incessant buzzing of cicadas broke the eerie silence. She leaned over and emptied the contents of her stomach on the ground.

She rummaged in her day pack for her water bottle. *Thank God I hadn't used the bottle before my fall.* She savoured a few mouthfuls, aware she would have to conserve her water.

Oh no, my bladder's full. How am I going to relieve myself when I can hardly move, let alone remove my clothing? 'Ahh!' She tried to move when shooting pains from her ribcage and groin immobilised her. She wanted to be sick again, and it dawned on her she must be dehydrated after lying in the sun all this time.

She had dressed right for the occasion in her baggy shorts, she thought, manoeuvring her way to the side of the cave entrance where the intense sun would soon take care of a puddle. After an agonising struggle, she managed to sort herself out.

Ah, that's a relief. At least it didn't happen when I was knocked out.

Fossicking through her bag again, she found a half-melted bar of chocolate, an apple and a high protein bar—snacks she would usually take on hikes. *Who knows how long this will have to last? Maybe I'll be here for weeks unless I'm never found.*

In a side pocket, she felt for her cell phone and turned it on. *Oh no, still no signal—at least I charged the battery this morning. Peter and Elly wouldn't have got my message that I wasn't meeting today. I should have told someone where I was going.*

Preparing for the worst, that it might be days, if not weeks before she is rescued, she decided to make a mattress after spying the available flora.

Crawling on her stomach, she edged her way back onto the ledge where she first fell. There was a large flax bush at her disposal, along with small tea tree bushes—just what she needed to build a soft mattress. She took her penknife from her pocket and tediously, under great duress, cut away at the flax leaves and tea tree branches, dragging bunches back and forth to the cave, congratulating herself on having kept the knife sharp for several years. It had been a gift from her late brother, Mark, who had died saving a drowning child at Piha.

It took repeated attempts to haul the branches that left her depleted of her dwindling strength. 'My body is broken,' she mumbled, her voice echoing against the rock walls. After making the perfect bed, she collapsed and lost consciousness.

When she awoke, thirst ripped her throat like something she hadn't experienced. *I'm dehydrating.* She rummaged around in her day pack for her drink bottle, savouring a few mouthfuls of the elixir of life.

Being a seasoned canyoner with the West Auckland Canyoning Club, she always came prepared for an emergency and had already consumed half of her ham sandwiches during the hike to the summit. She even carried a small first aid kit which held a packet of painkillers, and without delay, she swallowed two tablets with sparing sips of water. To still her pangs of hunger, she slowly consumed another sandwich, one cube of chocolate and a bite of the apple, careful to conserve what food she had left.

Oh, God, I don't want to spend the night in here. Please bring a search party or someone along this way, she begged in desperation, finding comfort in knowing she was not alone as she felt his divine presence with her.

Thinking that her flatmate, Briar and her two friends might be out searching for her, she crawled to the entrance of the cave again and called out, 'Help, please help—I'm here!' Her ailing voice disintegrated into the expansive oblivion of the sea. *It's useless! No one will hear me from here. I'm going to have to think of a way to attract attention*, she decided as the pills made her sleepy, causing her to drift off again.

When she woke this time, the sun had almost sunk below the horizon. There was not even the slightest tinge of a pink sunset as there usually was at the beach most summer evenings.

She cut extra tea tree to cover herself to keep her warm in the cave, as she knew from her canyoning experience that they can be cold places and she had to prepare for the night. The exertion exhausted her, and the pain returned soon after she had taken the painkillers, but it was too soon to take another dose, even though her head throbbed.

The bush descended into darkness and the moon appeared above the sea as a giant silver ball, providing her with light.

Her skin crawled as it dawned on her that creepy-crawlies hang out in caves, especially Wetas and large spiders. Perhaps tomorrow in the daylight she would have a better chance of drawing attention to herself. It will be Saturday and there'll be plenty of hikers and day-trippers out and about, she thought, trying to boost her dwindling morale.

The pain in her ribs and pelvis eased as the painkillers eventually did their job. She was a reluctant pill-popper and unaccustomed to using them, but she knew the dangers of shock and dehydration and needed to take care of herself.

She began to doze again, hoping to fall asleep, because that too would help her to heal.

As she drifted off, a strange sound drew her attention. Was she in another world or was this for real? Was that the sound of a boat engine chugging closer and closer? Irritated that she had just settled in for the night, she hauled her feeble body to the ledge again to investigate, momentarily ignoring the pain.

🐈 🐈 🐈

Manuel picked up his rucksack as the boat sped over the breakers into Whites Beach to drop him home. His bach stood hidden behind a clump of trees in the bush up a long track that eventually led to Anawhata beach. He would only stay there when on a drug run to remain incognito.

The sea was calm and easy to navigate. Carlos Rodriguez, the Brazilian drug lord who had several aliases and passports, had made sure they would only operate on a calm tide and a moonlit night. His swift, amphibious rib boat made short work of it.

Kingi took over the helm while his boss dipped into a metal box in the cabin and handed Manuel a plastic packet full of notes. 'This is your cut for the work you've done today—fair and square.'

Manuel's brows furrowed, not grasping what he had inferred by his remark and snatched the packet, counting the notes while holding a small penlight. He painstakingly tallied $3,000 in $100 bills.

'What's this? It's not all there! My cut should be $5,000, the same as Kingi's—that's what we agreed!'

Carlos roared at him. 'That's your cut mate plus a few grams to feed your habit or sell if you want. You didn't dive—Kingi did. You were only on standby as a backup in case something down there went wrong.'

'You told me you paid your divers $5,000 a mission. You didn't stick to the agreement. I would have done the job myself if I'd known this. It was just as risky if I had been caught on board by a coast guard.'

'I've given you what you're worth,' he muttered. 'Anyway, there's a bonus of nearly $1,000 worth of coke in that packet to feed your habit out of the kindness of my heart. You can sell that if you want.'

Was this an answer to prayer? Sandy was sure she saw a pale light from a boat on this bright, moonlit night. Yes, she was right. The boat lunged closer and slowed down as it neared the shallows. She wasn't sure what was happening. *What's going on? Fishermen, I suppose.* In the moonlight, she caught sight of the silhouette of fishing rods and three men. *That's it, now's my chance—perhaps the only one I get.* She picked up her phone and turned the light on. Thank God she had learnt how to send an SOS when she'd received training in advanced rock climbing.

She tried flicking her phone light on and off, aware of it draining her battery. 'Let me see … three short … three long … three short.' After signalling, she tried to shout, but her voice was as feeble as her body. 'Help me, please! Somebody help me.' The boat's engine and the noise of the surf drowned her cries.

One of the men in the boat appeared to tower over the others in the light of the moon, and he and a shorter fellow seemed to argue. The man at the helm must have seen Sandy's signal and pointed in her direction. The other men didn't look up, and the two continued their fracas while the waves on foreshore buffeted the boat. From where Sandy lay, the contenders waved their fists at each other in a heated dispute.

If only I could hear what they're saying. She strained to edge her way a little closer and stopped suddenly, fearing she could shoot over the edge.

She winced from the pain in her ribcage as she lay on her side. The only tolerable position for her was flat on her back, and that was not good—not right now.

Chapter Four

Manuel snatched the small packet of cocaine with a down-turned mouth and muttered quietly, 'There's nothing kind about you, mate!'

Without warning, while Manuel tucked his money and cocaine into his rucksack, Carlos, a six-foot-tall former heavy-weight boxer slammed his fist into the back of Manuel's head causing the man to hurtle over the side of the boat, his rucksack shooting across the deck.

'Darn fool! He should have shut up. Stop the engine—we'll have to get him back in the boat.'

Kingi guided the boat into the shallows and stopped the engine while he jumped into the bloodied water with Carlos, scooping up the body and throwing him back into the boat. Kingi bent over to assess the damage.

'He's still breathing—just unconscious. What are we going to do now? We've got kilos of crack onboard and an unconscious man. That was quite a smack in the head you gave him.'

'Well start he up and let's get going—we'll have to dump him overboard further out.'

Kingi's olive skin turned white as the colour drained from his face. 'What the heck are you talking about? He's still alive. You can't drown him—he hasn't done you any harm.'

Carlos ignored him and shoved him aside to take the wheel. 'Come on—get a move on. We'll have to offload him before the coastguard comes sniffing around, and get out of here, like you said,' snarled Carlos as he pushed his associate away from the steering wheel, revved the engine and took off. Kingi lurched forward, almost falling over the body, hurling his dreadlocks in all directions while Carlos glared at him.

Kingi eyeballed him back. 'Why did you have to bash him over the head? That's not what we discussed. I told you I didn't want to be a party to any killing and I'm not going back inside again—I made it clear. I only did a year, and I'm not going to be done for murder. That's life imprisonment!'

Carlos vented his temper ripping through the gears and thrusting the throttle open full speed heading out to the open sea.

Sandy changed her mind quickly about sending another SOS emergency signal and her stomach threatened to heave while she lay there, but the terrifying scene she had observed put her off. Now she deeply regretted drawing attention to herself and felt unsafe.

Her heart galloped as it pulsated in her throat. *Oh, no—is he dead?* She had seen the boat take off with only two men in it instead of three.

Don't tell me I'm a witness to a murder, especially when the thugs know I'm up here.

A blood-curdling shudder ran up her spine having witnessed the two men seizing the hands and feet of the limp body and slinging him like a sack of potatoes back into the boat and taking off.

They'll come looking for me later and finish me off too.

As if she didn't have enough stress to deal with, and now this.

To her relief, as she crawled back to the cave and collapsed onto her bed of greenery, she heard the engine sound grow faint as they disappeared into the dark abyss of the sea.

Nervous exhaustion and pain overwhelmed her. 'I hope the painkillers will get me through the night. I don't know how long they need to last.' She went off to sleep after praying words of desperation that the thugs would not come back for her.

🐐 🐐 🐐

'I call the shots and can change the terms of a deal at any time, especially if I think someone is going to be a liability,' Carlos snapped. 'I'm the one who takes the most risks transporting this stuff—and of course this time, so did you. Manuel was just there to give us back up and to be on guard when you were diving and removing the coke from the yacht's hull. At the end of the day, I didn't think he deserved a third share of the profit as he didn't dive, but I gave him a small supply of his own. That alone is worth nearly a grand. He was mighty ungrateful,' he said, sniffing loudly.

Kingi defended his mate, who lay slumped at his feet after Carlos had bound his legs with rope. 'I don't agree. They were the terms we had discussed with him, and to throw a spanner in the works at the last minute is not fair play. He was good to me in rehab, and I told him he could trust you. He's not using now—he has been clean since he left treatment.'

Carlos had never taken a risk like this before with a member of his drug ring. But he was sharp and would make sure that no one could ever prove he killed him. It was an accident, he'd say. Manuel lost his balance and fell overboard at sea. The only thing the police could accuse him of would be neglecting to inform the police of his death if he was ever caught.

He spat over the side of the boat as he slowed the engine a mile out from Whites Beach. 'Look, mate—it sounds like you need to pull your head in and stop wasting my time or I'll cut your rate too. Here—give me a hand to dump this waste of space over the side,' he growled.

Kingi was seething but said nothing as he grabbed the dead man under the arms while Carlos took his feet. They moved fast in case they received a visit from the coast guard. Tears stung Kingi's eyes as they slung his friend over the side. He knew that this would be the last time— his days of thuggery were at an end. He remembered the awards he had once received for bravery as a young man diving for the navy, and now he had become a criminal.

'We'd better make speed and get back to my vehicle before the coastguard catches us,' snapped Carlos.

'Well, I'm telling you again—this is the last time I get involved. I don't want blood on my hands and I can't trust you anymore. I've changed since I went into treatment and I don't want this life any longer.'

'Shut up—I don't want to hear your complaints. You should have thought about that before you'd agreed to do the job.'

Kingi perched on a deck seat, resting his face in his hands. He'd got in far too deep this time. Would Carlos leave him alone after this run? Perhaps it was too late for change. He would have to leave the country to get a fresh start.

It was a calm, windstill night and the bouncing of the boat on the waves almost lulled him to sleep. It had been a gruelling day, and he was desperate for it to be over. The money just wasn't worth the nerve-wracking risk when it went belly up.

He asked himself over and over why he had agreed to take up Carlos's offer of this diving job. Carlos knew he was one of the best divers they had come across with his exemplary skills gained from years of risky commercial diving for big money since he's left the navy. But now he was older, and since his short stint in prison for growing and selling cannabis, he had mellowed.

They disappeared into the night into Woodhill forest after disembarking on the beach where Carlos paid Kingi his dues.

'Thanks, it's all there,' said Kingi after he counted his money after stepping into the Ute.

'I've been thinking about the signal I saw on that cliff face at Whites Beach,' he said. 'We should have checked it out. From my navy experience, that was an SOS. Someone saw us. If Manuel was alive, he could have investigated, as it was not far from his bach. Someone may have been in trouble.'

Carlos spat on the ground. 'Oh, yeah—shall we call the police? Ridiculous! I didn't see any light. It was probably possum eyes shining in the dark—or larrikins playing in the bush. I have more important things on my mind!'

For the rest of the hour-long drive back to Carlos's mansion, one could cut the air with a knife, as no one spoke and Kingi was seething. Despite his boss's attempts at manipulation, Kingi was determined that once he got into his vehicle he left parked at Carlos's mansion, he would turn his back on Carlos Rodriguez, never to set eyes on him again if it were possible. But would Carlos leave him alone? He now had enough funds to start a new life far away. Carlos had convinced him to do this dive by threatening to harm his mother if he pulled out, but this time, Kingi would clear out and take his mother with him.

Carlos, the untouchable, returned to his high-security mansion in Fernhill. On a hilltop secluded in the bush, his estate stood fortified by high remote controlled gates and three Rottweiler dogs. This was just one of the multiple properties he kept around the world, and so far, he considered himself invincible. He didn't intend to be there long. Once he had shifted the cocaine to his regular customers in New Zealand, he would head off back to South America or another of his usual destinations and set about organising the next massive drug haul into New Zealand or Australia, the two countries that fetch the highest prices for this white gold.

As Kingi scrambled out of Carlos's Ute, relieved to be away from his tormentor, Carlos swung around and glared at him. 'Keep in touch,' he grunted, as Kingi climbed into his vehicle, ignoring him and driving off.

Chapter Five

Peter worried himself sick that night, wondering if anything untoward had happened to Sandy and had sent obsessive text messages to her and Elly, desperate for respite from his anguish.

He lived in hope that one day he would turn Sandy's head, but committed relationships were not on her agenda right now, he gathered, and he would have to settle for friendship. He guessed she'd never got over the love of her life, Carl Fielder, who'd jilted her for another woman two years earlier. He and Sandy had been engaged, and her sudden abandonment and humiliation was not something she was going to get over fast.

But Peter was not going to give up, not ever, from waiting, and wanting, and hoping, he had told her.

Finally, the phone rang at midnight and not a minute too soon. It was Sandy's flatmate.

'Hi, Briar—is she home—where did she say she'd been?' he said, trying to hide the desperation in his voice.

'No, sorry—I rang to say she hasn't returned. The strange thing is she never took her car, so someone else may have taken her into town to do some shopping or something.'

'It's so unlike her to forget to let one of us know. Unless she went swimming and got into trouble … oh, Briar—what shall we do?'

'I don't think the police will be interested if she hasn't been missing twenty-four hours. Even if she doesn't return tonight, they'll just say she stopped with a friend overnight.'

'We can't leave it longer than that. We'll have to report her missing, at least. I'll do it if you want.'

'No—leave it to me. It'll sound best coming from a flatmate. If she's not here in the morning, I'll go to the local police station. It's Saturday tomorrow—my day off.'

'Poor Sleuth will be wondering where she has got to if the black Labrador retriever is true to his name. Sandy usually walks him each day,' said Peter. 'I'll walk him—he knows me pretty well now. Let me know how you get on tomorrow.'

Peter came off the phone downcast. He couldn't bear the thought of anything bad happening to Sandy. Nothing ever seemed to go smoothly for him in his pursuit of happiness with this young woman who constantly rebuffed any attempt he'd made at romance. He suspected that her ex-fiancée, Carl, might be back on the scene since his current girlfriend, the one who took Sandy's place, had given him the big heave-ho. Sandy had told Peter that Carl had passed her on the beach a few times and asked if she was seeing anyone and they had a minor altercation over it.

Peter's emotional state sank even lower at the thought of having a rival together with Sandy's fear of commitment.

He took himself off to bed, thinking he should never have bolted down the burger and chips so late at night. Now, sleep would be a miracle.

🐾 🐾 🐾

Saturday Morning

Sandy had spent her first night alone in the cave in and out of consciousness, and the pain from her broken ribs and pelvis was unbearable. She was grateful she had always carried her small survivor kit with her on these hikes—a well-entrenched habit from her canyoning training. But strong painkillers barely scraped the surface of her pain now, and she had gone through half of her water supply.

A dark cloud of doom loomed over her as her eyes measured the scant water level in her drink bottle. How long could she go on like this? She knew from her rock climbing experience that people die from dehydration when in shock.

'Oh, no! Please—not that.' An insect had lodged itself under her tee-shirt, doing press-ups on her back. 'Ouch!' She ripped off her top and in the slim rays of the sun peeping into the cave, all she could see was a moth. It felt like sacrilege to let it go, her only vestige of companionship in this holocaustic nightmare. The creature struggled to free itself from her hand. 'Sorry, baby—I just wanted to hold you for a little while—off you go.' The moth took its chance at freedom and flew away. Sandy saw it settle on a clay rock nearby and took solace in that.

After a meagre breakfast of two bites of apple, a tiny piece of the protein bar and two cubes of chocolate, she embarked on her long, slow and bitterly painful journey out to the ledge. If she was to be discovered, it would not be hidden away in the cave. Now she would have to find a way to attract attention, but the ledge was pretty much hidden from view, even from Whites Beach.

She had an idea and painstakingly hauled off her tee-shirt to remove her red sports crop bra, then donned the top again. After she removed the small twigs from a long tea tree branch, she fastened the under-garment to it, forming a flag. Now all she needed to do was wait for someone to appear on the beach. But how would she know if it wasn't going to be one of the criminals she saw the previous night? She would have to be discerning and just wave it at swimmers or beach walkers.

It seemed like hours between lying down in the cave waiting for the light-headedness and nausea to subside and waving her crop bra at unsuspecting beach-goers who would probably see the flag as a prank. In between times, she tried her utmost to raise her voice to call for help. Saturday was usually a busier day on the beach and the track, but it seemed to no avail, as the weather would have put them off after the rain made the track muddy.

Sandy enjoyed her food and to have almost fasted for twenty-four hours made her fade, depleted of all energy. It made her voice weak so that she would never be able to make herself heard from that distance.

A heavy weight of disillusionment took her mind hostage. She was doomed.

Chapter Six

Elly had been up since the crack of dawn on Saturday morning and raced around to Sandy's house, as she and Peter had forgone their usual meeting on Lion Rock. She was dying to find out how Briar had got on with her local enquiries.

'Just in time for a coffee—I've just made one,' said Briar, offering Elly a seat at the dining table. She poured the coffee and passed her a small croissant.

'I'd love one—I'm on the afternoon shift today at the surf club and we're a waitress down so it's going to be busy this evening.'

'I just got back from the police station early this morning and filed a missing person report. They said they'll get the investigation underway, as Sandy has been missing more than twenty-four hours. They'll contact LandSAR, the Land Search and Rescue.'

'Have you tried her parents? They might know something.'

'Yes, I have and they haven't heard from her for a few weeks. Now they are worried sick,' said Briar.

'Poor things. I suppose they'll find out soon as it will be all over the news media. I thought she may have gone to Piha Falls on her scooter. That's the track she usually likes to walk.'

'No, her scooter is still in the garage—so is her car. Whatever she has done, she has gone on foot or taken off with a friend in their vehicle,' said Briar, handing her another croissant.

'It's as though she has disappeared from thin air. I asked around at the surf club and her art group and no one has heard from her.' Elly leaned on the table with her elbow, resting her face in her hand.

'Don't worry, Elly. Knowing Sandy, she has gone to stay with a mate and forgotten to tell you and Peter. She could have left her cell phone somewhere—that's why we're not receiving her text messages.'

'I guess so,' muttered Elly.

'It appears Peter was the last one to see her. He and Sandy went for a walk along the beach until late the night before she went missing. It was that lovely warm evening with a huge moon—so romantic. I had gone to bed before she came home and don't know what time she returned.'

Elly picked up her sunhat and glasses and headed for the door with Briar in tow. 'Yes, I heard. But I think that romance was far from her mind, according to Peter.'

'I hear that jerk Carl has been trying to get back on the scene again after he cheated on her,' said Briar. 'Who does he think he is?'

'Yeah, I know. Sandy told me he went into a rage when she told him to get lost. He thinks she and Peter are in a relationship.'

Briar stood with her hands on her hips, grimacing. 'Well, it's a bit too late for him to react now—that horse has bolted!'

'I'd like to be involved with the search and rescue—how about you?' Elly asked.

'Yes, I'm in too and I'm sure Peter will join us.'

'Thanks for the coffee and croissants, Briar. Let's keep in touch.'

'I will do. Peter said he'll call later and I'll fill him in—bye for now.'

🐈 🐈 🐈

Kingi pulled over to the side of the road to take a call on his disposable mobile. The only person who should be contacting him on that phone should be Carlos. He checked the caller ID and reluctant as he was, he answered the call.

'Carlos—what's up?'

'I thought you would have been in contact to touch base,' he said, with a resentful tone.

'Sorry, mate, been busy sorting my life out.'

'Well, I hope it involved checking out the source of that SOS signal you saw that night. Haven't you heard the news about that Piha woman going missing in that area? It was probably her.'

'Yes, I heard. But if it is her, she is a friend and I won't do her any harm.'

'What?' Carlos screeched through the phone. 'What do you mean you know her?'

'She was my caseworker and counsellor at rehab and also Manuel's and went out of her way to help me and my family.'

'Oh, is that right? You'd better help me and make sure she isn't going to be a key witness to a murder, or you'll implicate yourself as an accessory.'

Kingi wanted to hang up the phone but was careful not to aggravate him.

'We'll have to wait and see if they find Manuel's body and go from there. I'll be in touch again. Keep your phone handy,' he ordered and hung up.

Chapter Seven

Peter answered the phone. It was Elly with an update.

'Did you get my voice message I left about the search?'

'Yes, but I didn't understand what you meant that they were starting today.'

'Briar said the police will work with LandSAR, the Land Search and Rescue volunteers and start looking at the south end of the beach this afternoon, working their way through the bush in three stages and end at Whites Beach. If you're still joining them, you'll have to be at the surf club at 11 am today where the police and volunteers will meet with the search party to give them their schedule before they go out.'

'I hope to be there—what about you?'

'I can't get the day off work, not for the lack of trying. I've run out of leave and they're short-staffed in the restaurant. I finish at three. You go and tell me all the news tonight.'

'Sure, I will. I'd better get ready then—I'm running behind.'

Peter hung the phone up and checked his diary. He was in a bind as he had a major contract to complete for a client and really could not afford the time. His architectural business in the area was flourishing due to the increase in city dwellers moving out to the beaches and bushy areas. But he owed it to Sandy to help find her and he would have it on his conscience if he didn't make an effort.

Before he left the house, he received another call—this time from a detective saying that he needed to talk to him regarding his relationship with Sandy. He was shocked that they would want to question him.

'Detective Inspector, Alexander Crawford is the name, but you can call me Al—everyone else does. I'll drop by your home at around 6 pm this evening if that's okay.'

'I'll be at the meeting for the search party this morning.'

'That's no problem. I'll be there too, but I'll meet you at your home at six. We're talking to other people in the area who know Sandy Barrett and doing house to house enquiries.'

'Well make sure you talk to that jerk of an ex-fiancée who has been hassling her.'

Al hung up the phone, obviously not wanting to discuss the issue over the phone.

Peter was shaken up by the fact that the police wanted to question him. Perhaps he was overreacting as they were probably visiting all the residents in the area, he told himself, but he would be the last person to harm her. He also felt a tad guilty about mentioning Carl to him—perhaps that was unfair.

The search parties met at the surf club as arranged where they handed out the schedules and rosters to the volunteers.

Peter attended the meeting and returned home to carry on with his work. He had to finish a large contract for a local developer which he didn't want to lose as competition in that area was fierce.

He sat in his office and glanced at the search schedule out of curiosity. The first day of the search the police and tracker dogs accompanied by local volunteer LandSAR people would strategically scan the beach and bush right out to Mercer Bay. If Sandy was still not found, they would continue searching the whole of the Piha area systematically.

On Sunday they would start in Piha central and the track out to Piha Falls where

Sandy often when walking. Day three, on Monday they were scheduled to search the bush in North Piha out to Whites Beach.

When he finished reading through the document, stomach acid rose to his throat. The reality that his best friend was missing suddenly impacted him and he began to feel it was the wrong thing for him to go on the search. Imagine them finding her body while he is there—he just wouldn't be able to take it.

He decided he would rather bury himself in his work and catch up with the updates from Briar who said she would take time off work to attend the rescue party all week.

🐾 🐾 🐾

Day one of the search, tracker dogs and police had led the party for the whole day in Kare Kare and at the Mercer Loop in the rain. It was a messy business with the bush so wet, but today it had turned to light showers, although more heavy rain had been forecast. This first day of the search, they were unsuccessful in finding any clues to her whereabouts.

That afternoon, Peter and Elly met for a drink at the surf club with a few of the people they knew from the search party who had finished their shift at 3 pm. Soaking wet

39

raincoats and jackets hung from the hooks at the front door of the club.

After he and Elly questioned the volunteers about the search, Peter sat with his head in his hands with Elly rubbing his back to console him.

'Don't despair, Peter. There's a lot more bush to search yet. Something will turn up that will give them clues. Sandy always goes well-prepared if she goes out hiking.'

'Well, I hope they won't find her in the bush unless she is alive. I had a call from a detective today who wants to meet me at home at six. He said they may want to bring me into the station for questioning and with my consent they're searching my house right now taking my cell phone and laptop for inspection. He asked me to stay in Piha and not leave until I have been cleared, as I'm a person of interest to the police.'

Elly looked aghast, her cheeks losing their high colour.

'What—you must be joking. You are one of her best friends! How did he deduce that?'

He cleared his throat. 'Because I was the last person seen with her the night before she went missing. A few residents saw me with her too, including Briar.'

Elly's eyes grew larger. She saw how gaunt his face had become the last few days and placed an arm around his shoulders.

'They have nothing to pin on you, Peter. They need concrete evidence.'

Peter slumped in his seat, leaning forward on his elbows with his face in his hands. He shook his head. 'You don't understand, Elly. Right now the cops are going through my home looking high and low for dirt on me, I'm sure.'

'Oh—are they going to give back your phone and laptop afterwards?'

'Yeah—they said they'll return them when they've finished their examination. It's a real pain, as I need them for my business and told them that.' His voice was hollow.

Peter trudged down the steps despairing that Sandy would have to spend another night wherever she was and whatever misfortune had her in its grip.

When he arrived home, he was surprised to see his house looking so tidy after the police had searched. They had taken his laptop and phone which he had left on the dining table for them. He guessed they treated him with the respect he deserved because he had been more than cooperative. Apart from a few drawers still left open, they had left it at as they'd found it. Peter was grateful he chose to live in a minimalistic home and there was little for them to inspect.

Al turned up at 6 pm to make his enquiries. He stood tall on Peter's doorstep looking more like a slick salesman than a detective in his white, Brixton Messer Fedora hat, beige trousers and brown slip-on boots. He also wore a rather flowery shirt for a police officer, Peter thought.

He ushered him to a seat in the lounge. 'Can I offer you tea or coffee—or perhaps a cold drink?'

'Tea with milk, no sugar would be fine, thanks.'

While Peter made the tea, he spied Al having a good poke around his lounge, scanning the items on his shelves.

He returned and handed him a mug of tea.

'So you didn't join the search party, I hear—did I frighten you off?' Al's piercing blue eyes looked right through him.

'The thing is—Sandy's flatmate told me you were probably the last person to see her the night before she disappeared. She said you both went for a walk along the beach until late.'

Unintimidated, Peter answered confidently, 'Ah, yes—the moon was so bright and the beach all lit up—a warm night and too uncomfortable to sleep. We had a long talk.'

Al's bushy eyebrows snapped together. 'Romantic walking along the beach in the moonlight, was it? And I guess she wasn't having a bar of it.'

Peter glared at him. 'Yes ... it was a beautiful evening ... but it wasn't like that! We just had a long talk, that's all. We made a small fire at the north end of the beach by those little caves and toasted marshmallows until nearly midnight.'

'What did you do after that—did you go straight home?'

'Yes—after I walked her back to her house first. When I arrived home, I noticed the neighbour's bedroom light was still on, so you can check my alibi with her.'

'And Sandy didn't mention what she had planned the next day?'

'We usually meet each morning at the top of Lion Rock for fellowship around nine and I guess she clean forgot to tell me she had other plans for that morning. I expected her to send a text message when she didn't turn up.'

Peter sat nervously pulling on his finger socket joints.

'Look—you've got the wrong end of the stick. We're not in a relationship—just good friends from home church.'

'So what was the long talk about?'

'She was discussing her ex-fiancée, Carl Fielder who has tried to get back after cheating on her and now making a nuisance of himself.'

'Mmm—I suppose we'll be asking him a few questions too.'

Al had let his tea go cold and having realised it, grabbed the cup and gulped it down all at once.

'Are you sure she didn't mention she was meeting a friend or going into town?'

'I'm sorry, Al—I'd like to be able to help you, believe me, but she didn't say a word about that. Apart from telling me about Carl, she said she had a new painting in progress and told me all about it.'

'Of course—I hear she is a budding young artist and doing well in the area. Is that her art gallery on Marine Parade with a good view of Lion Rock?'

'Yep—that's her pride and joy. She and Briar share the house and Sandy's parents own it. They are pretty wealthy and have several other houses on the coast. Her father owns that huge advertising company, Barrett and Co in the Auckland Central Business District.'

'Interesting icon this Lion Rock,' Al said pointing at the huge rock looming high in front of Peter's house on Marine Parade.

'Yep, sure is. Do you know why they call it Lion Rock?' Peter asked him.

'Nope, no idea. From this vantage point, I can't see any resemblance to a Lion.'

'No—but take a look at this.' Peter directed him into his office to show him a large photograph that had been shot from the rear of the hundred-metre tall rock.

Al shoved his hands into his trouser pockets and scanned the image. 'Ah—now I see it. Looks like a lion alright.'

'It's a male lion lying down. Cool, isn't it?'

'Yep, certainly is—great photo. Thanks for that information.' He turned and moved towards the front door. 'Well, that's all the questions I have for now—thanks for the tea. We may need you for more questioning, so stay in the area until our enquiries have finished, please.'

'Does that make me a suspect? I hope not.'

Al stopped short as he headed for the door. 'Well, I hope not too—are you?' he said, with a wry smile.

'No way!—Sandy is the last person on earth I would want to harm. Please—just find her,' he said, as his voice broke up.

Peter rushed up to him suddenly. 'Wait! There is something else you need to know ... at least ... I think it's important.'

Al leaned his back against the doorpost looking wide-eyed at Peter. 'Go ahead.'

'A man stalked Sandy a while back and gave her the jitters, but she hasn't seen him since.'

'Where was this—at home?'

'Yes—he was a client at the rehab where she worked as an addiction counsellor. That was her occupation before she took up writing columns for a woman's health magazine and selling paintings. She's a qualified psychologist.'

'So what happened with this bloke?'

Peter directed him back inside. 'You'd better sit down. Come back into the lounge.'

Al sat with his mouth half open, desperate for whatever evidence he could extract from Peter who was just as frantic to have the heat removed from himself.

'At one of our meetings on Lion Rock, Sandy confided in Elly and me that she mistakenly let slip to a client in recovery that she lived on Piha beachfront. He asked her about the best walking tracks around Piha and she told him about the ones that were her favourites. When she heard that he had left the treatment centre and had returned to crime, she told us how frightened she was and that she regretted telling him anything about herself.'

'That's interesting. When did she think he had started stalking her?'

'About two weeks before she went missing. She said he only appeared once in front of her house, but it was enough to unnerve her.'

'So this doesn't prove that he was stalking her—he could have had various other reasons for being on the beach. Maybe he had been to the shop or just wanting to swim at Piha that day. Many people pass her house to get to the beach as they would yours. I guess she didn't mention his name.'

'She couldn't break confidentiality so she was unable to tell us his name. You could ask Briar—she may know more. I can give you the name of the centre—it was *Living Free* in Cornwallis.'

Al jotted it down and poked his notebook back into his pocket. 'Okay, Peter. I'll investigate this further—thanks for your cooperation. Hopefully, we can identify him first and then make some enquiries. I'll be in touch.'

After the detective left, Peter was just in time to catch the last of the weather forecast and to burst his bubble, even more, it forecast rain later that night. *Poor Sandy—if she is lost out there somewhere—imagine in the bush in the cold and rain all alone.* He began to feel a sense of impending doom at the possibility of a hardened criminal and drug dealer seeking her out. It didn't bear thinking about. Instead, he prayed for her safe return.

His head was in a spin over everything that was happening and he decided to take Sleuth for a walk along the beach. Although it was his usual dinner time, he'd lost his appetite and needed to do some serious thinking. Briar wasn't at home but she'd agreed he could walk the dog at any time. A delicious aroma emanated from the kitchen as he walked around to Sleuth's kennel.

He took a stroll along the beach with the dog on a lead. When he reached the lagoon by the domain, he unclipped him to let him run around away from beachgoers.

Within a short time, Peter could see the dog was bored hanging around the lagoon and knew how much he enjoyed bounding in the waves on the seashore, so he moved on and headed towards the dog designated area where he could unleash him.

As soon as they arrived, Sleuth took off into the sea, lurching at the shallow waves as they broke on the seashore. Peter smiled as he watched him making nose dives at the seagulls and thanked his maker that the dog was oblivious to the tragedy that had befallen his beloved owner. Sleuth shook his drenched coat over Peter's legs while he bent to clip the lead back onto his collar and prepare to return home. Sleuth pulled away suddenly, tripping Peter up, and bounded up the beach towards the steps leading onto Laird Thomson Track, the one that Sandy had taken that led to the lookout.

'Hey, not that way. I'm not going up there—I'm way too unfit for a huge hike. Come back here, Sleuth!' He chased after the excited dog, frantic to get him back on the lead. *Why is he so keen to go up the track? Perhaps he's got a scent of another animal up there or maybe it's a sign he's stressed.*

When he caught him up, he bent down to pick up a piece of driftwood and threw it towards the water. 'Go, boy—fetch it for me!'

He continued to hurl the stick into the waves until Sleuth realised he wasn't playing his game and ran into the water. The dog retrieved it and dropped it at Peter's feet who quickly grabbed his collar and attached the lead.

'Good boy—well done.'

As they walked back home, Peter felt a degree of comfort knowing that this animal was

Sandy's best friend and he sensed that he had a part of her with him when they were together.

Briar had already arrived home and Peter found her in the kitchen preparing a meal.

'Hi, mate. Just in time for dinner—please join me,' she said.

The aroma from the kitchen rekindled his appetite.

'That's kind of you—are you sure? You weren't expecting me.'

'I know it's late, but we both have to eat and I always keep extra in case my friends drop in.' Briar handed him the packet of dog pellets. 'Mind feeding him for me first? He'll need water too and then we can eat—it's almost ready.'

'Mmm—smells good—sure, won't be long.'

'Before you arrived, I just popped along the beach to the shop while the roast was cooking to get milk and there are police everywhere making enquiries. I got a phone call earlier to say that a police officer will come to my house tomorrow after the search to ask more questions.'

They sat down to a substantial meal of roast chicken and Greek salad with boiled potatoes, swapping notes about their day. After telling Briar about the discussion the DI had with him, he grilled her about the rehab client.

'We have to give him some useful information to start with and if you can remember everything Sandy told you about him, it might help the police identify him. I feel he seems determined to pin the crime on me, for some reason.'

'I can do better than that—I was at home with her that day and she pointed the guy from the rehab out to me. I still remember what he looked like as he looked sinister and gave me the creeps.' She passed him the salad. 'I remember specifically that he had a kind of chain tattoo around his neck and one on his ankle and wore his hair in dreads. I thought for an ex-con he scrubbed up well—had an attractive face and olive skin.'

'Wow! That's going to be useful. There aren't many people these days who wear dreadlocks in this neck of the woods—what else can you remember?'

'She couldn't disclose his name, but after we saw him hanging around, Sandy told me a bit more about him. Apparently, he got some woman pregnant, and she kicked him out because of his anger issues. He started making good progress in making amends and dealing with his problems and then after a few months, he crashed and left the centre. Sandy heard from colleagues that he went back using and into crime.'

Peter took a ciabatta roll and buttered it. 'Well, I think you'd better talk to Detective Inspector Crawford who came to see me—especially if he was hanging around your house after she told him where she lives.'

After the meal, they sat in the covered porch talking about possible reasons Sandy hadn't returned.

'I'm beginning to worry now, Peter. She obviously didn't go off with a friend into town or stay with someone overnight. She would always tell me if she wasn't going to come home at night. It's a kind of pact we had to keep each other safe.'

'I guess the only other explanation is that she has gone off for a hike somewhere and got lost. She told me she has been lost in the bush a few times and on one occasion, Sleuth guided her back home when he was with her.'

Peter's eyes narrowed. 'There's only one other possibility, a more sinister one,' he said, clearing his throat.

'I suppose you know that Sandy's parents are loaded—I mean they are extremely wealthy and some thug may have taken her hostage—like that bloke from the rehab if he got back into crime. That's what worries me—they may have planned to kidnap her for a ransom and it could have gone wrong and they harmed her.'

'Oh, Briar—you're letting your imagination run wild. Sandy's clever and can take care of herself,' he said, with a quaver in his voice, trying to convince himself. What she said just sickened him.

Briar refrained from deepening that discussion when she saw his face drop.

'I'd best be getting home now. I've got a hefty contract to finish this week. Please let me know if you hear any news. The meal was outstanding and I'll return the favour sometime soon.'

Briar could see he was upset as he went out the door. He wasn't prepared to face the reality that something very sinister had caused Sandy's disappearance—he just couldn't cope with that yet.

'Looks like you're just in time. I think that rain is going to set in,' Briar said ducking under the cover of the porch.

The light shower of rain began to turn heavier as a crack of thunder boomed across the valley preceded by flashes of lightning on the sea's horizon. Peter shuddered at the thought of Sandy being trapped somewhere on a blustery,

wet night. On the way home to his house along
Marine Parade, he prayed for her protection.

Chapter Eight

Was that rain she could hear? The weather had been scorching hot since her fall and now she welcomed things to cool down. But how waterproof will her temporary home be?

As the shower turned into heavy rainfall, the cave started dripping until tiny rivers ran down the rocks into her hiding place. By some miracle, the water tracked into channels at the side of the cave, but not where she lay so that her bed of branches stayed dry.

Quickly she grabbed her drink bottle that had barely a few sips of live-saving water left and placed it under the larger of the mini torrents. 'Thank you God!' she bellowed. She was so proud she had carefully conserved her water and now she could relax.

How will they find me now in this heavy rain?

She had also spared her phone battery, turning it off during the day and using it only at night when necessary. Weakness had set in due to the pain which she treated with rest. Her debilitation caused her to stop waving her red underwear on the stick, as she no longer had the strength to crawl backwards and forwards to the ledge or to hold up the stick.

At times, when she drifted off to sleep she was afraid it was the end of the road and she wouldn't wake up again. At those times she prayed that God's will be done and committed her life into his hands.

Tonight was darker than the previous nights she had spent in the cave. A full moon had shone into her space but now it was pitch black as she lay back with her head on her backpack listening to the silence of the bush. Usually, she would hear the comforting sound of a morepork and cicadas, but tonight there was nothing but unnerving wind and rain.

She shivered as the outside temperature dropped and for the first time she needed her anorak at the bottom of her backpack. For this she was grateful and the thick lining provided enough warmth to get her through a cold night with it zipped up to her chin. The dry tea tree branches were adequate to cover her legs.

Recollections of the walk on the beach she had shared with Peter flashed forefront in her mind for some reason. She visualised his kind face—handsome with thick black hair he kept with short back and sides. Although she couldn't admit to herself that they were in a relationship, she was attracted to him. Not only his looks but his heart and soul kept him in her life.

What is he doing now that I'm missing? He must be frantic. What about poor Sleuth, my darling boy? He'll wonder where I've gone too.

'Please God, please bring me back home—make a way where there seems to be no way.'

As the rain pelted down on the rocks above, the sound lulled her into a deep sleep.

🐾 🐾 🐾

Sunday

The finishing touches to the expansive bush property development he had designed for his latest customer had taken Peter's mind off Sandy for the interim.

He turned the television on just in time to hear the 6 pm news. As usual, Sandy's disappearance was in the headlines and it took him all the mental strength he could muster to listen to the announcement about the failed search. Grief overtook him as he reached to turn off the TV when a breaking news flash caught his attention. The police believed that the death of the Brazilian who had been found by fishermen on Keyhole Rock on Auckland's West coast that afternoon may be linked to the disappearance of Sandy Barrett who disappeared two days ago.

Peter's blood curdled. Surely that wasn't a coincidence. Police couldn't comment on whether they believed the man had drowned, or it had been a suspicious death but forensics had estimated the time of death had been in the last twenty-four hours.

Peter's morose mood returned as he turned the TV off. A warm shower and a spruce up with the new shirt his sister bought him for Christmas and trendy coordinating garments made him feel better. Perhaps eating something different from his usual boring stir-fries might enable him to cope with the grim news.

Tomorrow he must contact Al and find out if the dead man could be connected to Sandy in any way, but for now, he was desperate to find anything to take his mind off it all. It was almost 8 pm and Elly had invited Peter for a meal at the Surf Club on her evening off to cheer him up. He rummaged through his wardrobe looking for something better than the clothes he had been wearing since Sandy's disappearance. Most days he just couldn't be bothered attending to himself at all with his mind in such a whir. But tonight he would make an extra effort to spruce himself up so as not to embarrass one of Sandy's best friends. He looked forward to an uplifting evening with a kind friend, as lately things had started to drag him down. He needed someone to distract him from the increasing macabre events that had taken his mind hostage.

🐈 🐈 🐈

It was Carlos again, and this time Kingi felt like stamping on his phone.

'So they've found Manuel's body. Didn't take long for it to wash up on the rocks, although it's been half-eaten and almost unidentifiable.'

'I know, I listen to the news,' Kingi mumbled.

'Well, I'm letting you know I'm clearing out of here and joining my crew ready for the next haul. I know you said you won't be in on it, but you'd better speak up now if you've changed your mind.'

'No, mate. I've got family to think about. I'm done with all the drama now.'

'So it appears you might be right about that Piha girl being a witness. I'm leaving you to take care of it if you want to stay out of prison.'

'I told you I won't harm her. If it was her, she wouldn't have been able to see much from

59

up on the cliff. It probably was just larrikins acting the fool.'

Well for your sake, you'd better be right. If you need to get hold of me, you know what to do, but destroy that phone of yours now,' he snarled and hung up.

Chapter Nine

There was a loud knock at the door. Peter squinted at his watch face that appeared a blur. *Who's this so early in the morning?* His head ached and already he felt the tension in his body return.

He threw on a dressing gown. 'Hang on, I'm coming!' he yelled with annoyance, dying for a sleep in after staying at the club until late and walking Elly home. He peered again at his watch. 'What? 7 am—feels like ten,' he muttered as he staggered to the door.

Al loomed large as Peter opened the door with one hand shielding his eyes from the bright sunlight squeezing its way through the ominous clouds.

The detective held Peter's laptop case in one hand. 'Sorry, mate. I thought you might like to hear the results of your house search yesterday.'

'Come on in—breakfast? I could rattle up some eggs if you like.'

'No, thanks all the same. I've already eaten.'

'Come and sit down. If you don't mind I'll put the kettle on. I'm dying for my mug of coffee to start the day,' said Peter as he took the laptop Al handed to him.

The DI dug into his jacket pocket and pulled out Peter's phone. 'Here's your cell phone. Look, mate—sorry about the intrusion, but you must understand—the sooner we can eliminate innocent parties from our enquiries the easier it will be to narrow down the real suspects.'

'You mean I'm no longer under suspicion?'

'No, I'm not saying that at all. It's just that we found no incriminating evidence in your house or on your devices and have character witnesses alleging you are a pillar of the community. Therefore we have no reason to detain you as a suspect for now.'

Peter's down-turned mouth and furrowed brow made him look more dejected than ever. 'So what do you want from me to prove I haven't harmed her?'

'I suppose, unless you can find her, you'll just have to sit tight and let us do our job trying to discover her whereabouts and whether there has been any foul play.'

'Well, I wish you'd all get a move on as the suspense is killing me!' Peter snapped.

'I think it is Sandy you should be giving more thought to and not yourself, don't you think?'

Although Al's remark irritated him it also convicted him that he was acting as though he was the victim, when all this time Sandy could be suffering intolerable terror and pain.

'So—are you going to tell me about this bloke who drowned and was found at Keyhole Rock? Please don't keep me in the dark about that. Do you think it's connected?'

'Sorry—naturally the body is with the coroner and we can't release any information to the public, even if I did know more. There will be a news release once the restraints are removed.'

'I'm not just anyone, am I?'

'I realise that—but no one said it was a drowning. It is likely to be a suspicious death and you'll have to wait until we can release the coroner's findings.'

'I hope it wasn't a kidnap plan for Sandy gone wrong,' Peter mumbled, his voice quavering.

'It's a possibility that we'll have to look into I'm afraid because of the timing of Sandy's disappearance and this body turning up.'

'What? I was just casually surmising. Do you think it is a possibility?'

'I can't discuss it further, but we will investigate this death to see if he can be linked in some way to Sandy, seeing it coincided with her disappearance.'

'I feel ill at the thought of her being kidnapped. Poor Sandy.' Peter summoned every bit of self-control to blink back the tears that formed in his eyes. Al must have seen it and picked up his sunhat, making a move towards the front door.

'Are you searching Elly's house too?'

'No—she has an alibi.'

'Oh, that's right. She stayed with a friend at Wood Bay on her days off and was going to arrive home late the night before she disappeared. I guess her friend can vouch for that.'

'Her brother confirmed that she came home late that night,' Al replied.

He picked up his hat and keys as he walked to the door. 'I'll keep you informed. Thanks for cooperating,' he said, bounding down the path to his car.

The minute he left, Peter broke down. The floodgates opened and his tears made a mess of his office desk which he wiped away before they damaged the portfolio he needed to take to his customer later in the day. He was bursting to phone Elly and Briar to ask if they'd heard the news about the body found at Keyhole Rock, but Briar would already be with the search party in Piha central and Piha Falls according to the schedule. Elly would be sleeping in after working late the night before.

He decided there was still time to take Sleuth out for a walk, before the dog curfew. Poor animal, h*ow he must be missing Sandy and can't talk about his anguish like I can. A good play on the beach will do him good.* He looked at the dark sky and removed his nylon parka from the hook, hoping the rain would hold out.

As Peter walked up the path towards Sandy's gate, Sleuth bounded up to the fence, his tail wagging madly as though he'd been waiting for his next walk.

'Gidday, fella,' said Peter, as the dog nearly knocked him over, stretching up high to lick his face. 'Down boy! I've already washed this morning. Come on—let's get your lead.'

The dog scampered around the side of the house to the garden shed where the girls kept his gear. On the way there, Peter turned on the hose and topped up the dog's water basin before securing the lead to his collar.

'I suppose you want to go to the unleashed area, but first, you have to stay on the lead.'

The dog trotted happily along the side of the road and pulled Peter down the track onto the dunes north of Lion Rock.

'Come on, boy. Let's blow out the cobwebs.' Peter had Sleuth on a long, running leash that Sandy used when she took him out for a run along the beach. Although he was no long-distance runner, he enjoyed jogging along the beach but had trouble keeping up with Sleuth who almost tugged him over a few times.

They reached the designated, unleashed dog area where Peter was relieved to unclip the animal's lead and rest his hand.

Sleuth began chasing the foam on the shallow waves as Peter continued running up the beach towards Barnett Hall. When they arrived there, he sat down to catch his breath and suck in the sea air. Looking above at the threatening clouds forming again, he calculated how much time they had.

'Okay buster, we'd better go before we catch a deluge,' He said, leaning over to grab hold of Sleuth's collar. The dog wrenched away from Peter's grip, almost toppling him, and bounded away up the beach heading north.

'Get back here, you hyena!' he bellowed, panicking. 'Sleuth get here!' He looked around, but no one was up that end of the beach, to his relief.

Sleuth just kept running, but Peter caught up to him. He took hold of his collar and while he picked up the lead to find the clip, the animal yanked hard and was off again. They were at the far car park and Peter wanted to take another break but knew unleashed dogs weren't permitted at the far end of the beach to protect the penguins and other wildlife.

'This will be the last time I let you off the leash in North Piha,' Peter mumbled.

He hauled himself up taking to his heels after the defiant animal which once again, headed for Laird Thomson track. This dog was determined to get him into trouble.

Sleuth raced up the steps and halted towards the top, waiting for Peter with his bright eyes enlarged and tongue hanging out as he panted with excitement.

'Wait, boy. Come on, please, Sleuth— don't run off again.'

But Peter guessed the dog thought it was some kind of game of cat and mouse. His trainers skidded in the mud on one of the steps near the top that were washed out after the previous night's heavy rain. 'Darn animal bringing me up here in these conditions.'

He was worried he would be reported and fined for having a dog on a track where they are banned. Now he began to get angry, despite having great affection for Sandy's canine friend.

As Peter walked up to him, the dog appeared to stop and wait, and Peter hoped his game was over. 'Stupid mutt, come here!' he called.

The dog whined, turned and galloped on ahead up the muddy track through the bush with Peter in close pursuit, finally reaching the lookout at the summit. Peter saw his mood change suddenly and his heart sank as he watched him looking towards the sea whimpering with his tail between his legs and ears drooping.

'What is it, fella? Have you been up here before? I doubt it.'

Peter couldn't work it out as the council stopped people walking their dogs on this track and others where the wildlife was endangered and Sandy would be the first one to reinforce the rules. *So what is the magnet that pulls him up here?*

Peter quietly talked to Sleuth and got close enough to grab hold of his collar. 'Gotcha!

Let's get this lead back on you and go back down before we get into trouble.'

Once he secured the dog, he hesitated and thought he should first have a good look around while they were up there. He couldn't see anything untoward at the lookout. He wondered if he should start calling Sandy's name and then decided he must be delusional. As far as he knew, Sandy never spoke of walking this track. She mainly stuck to Piha Falls where she would ride her bike to the track, or she would walk with Sleuth to Taitomo Island in South Piha outside the curfew.

The dog's behaviour had been strange. Perhaps Briar could shed some light on it.

As he arrived at the bottom of the steps from the lookout, LandSAR had arrived and gave him a right rollicking for being in a cordoned area where they were beginning their search. He should have known better, and they cautioned him before he took off back to Briar's house.

🐕 🐕 🐕

Monday

The cave was already in darkness. Sandy was sure she'd heard a man's voice echoing across the bush-covered valley. If only she had the voice to yell out, but she could barely verbalise anything.

It might be those men from the boat coming to look for me? She daren't try to attract attention. Drifting in and out of sleep, she prayed that she would soon be rescued. She knew the search parties were thorough, as she had taken part in rescues numerous times over the years, most of them successful. But for now, all she wanted to do was sleep and stay comfortable. She was set for the night and as it began to rain, she placed her drink bottle under a tiny stream that began to run down a crevice in the rock wall at the blind end of the cave. At least she'd have enough water to keep her going for another few days.

🐕 🐕 🐕

When Peter arrived back at Briar's house with Sleuth in the pouring rain, he was disappointed she was not home. He desperately wanted to tell her about the dog's strange behaviour at the lookout. Perhaps it was a rabbit that had drawn his attention and he had picked up its scent the first time he ran up there. Peter knew he loved chasing rabbits—the makings of a true retriever.

He guessed he was overreacting to the dog's behaviour and let it go, but could still mention it to Briar in passing.

Elly phoned his mobile to say that Briar was with her and would he like to drop over for coffee. She was on the early shift and had finished work.

'Sure, I'll come right over.'

He grabbed his parka and wasted no time in walking around to Elly's house to catch up on the updates.

'Anything turn up on the search today?' Peter asked, pouring himself a plunger coffee.

'Nothing—no clues or belongings found. I must say it was messy and difficult poking around in all the slush and puddles,' said Briar. 'Thick mud had washed over the path making it slippery and hard to walk up the steps and through the bush.'

Peter's face lit up. 'That can only be a good thing. I hope they don't find anything. There's always a chance she is still alive if the searches are unsuccessful.'

Peter was dying to tell the women about the trouble he had with Sleuth at the lookout. After he spewed it out, Briar had the answer.

'Didn't you know about Sandy's latest venture? She registered Sleuth with the Conservation Dog's Program for training to protect monitored birds and to spot pests that put our native wildlife at risk. She is also receiving dog handling training.'

'I remember she did mention something at one of our meetings on Lion Rock that she had joined some program with the Department of Conservation,' said Peter.

Elly handed them each a muffin. 'Oh yeah, that's right, but I didn't know it involved Sleuth.'

'She didn't want to say too much until she was an accredited dog handler with DOC,' said Briar. 'Some of the locals here could get obnoxious if they learnt she was able to take her dog on the restricted tracks. That's just an ignorant attitude though.'

Peter looked relieved. 'Well, that explains it. He must have detected a pest or protected species up there and was frustrated I wouldn't let him track it. It must have confused him, poor Sleuth.'

'Anyway—that aside, has anyone news about the identity of the chap found on Keyhole Rock yet?' asked Elly.

Peter slurped his coffee. 'I'll chase it up. I need to speak to Al about a few things so I'll see if I can get hold of him tonight.'

For a few minutes, there was silence. Peter's face appeared tense again. 'So what will happen if they don't find her tomorrow when they cover North Piha, Briar?' His voice shook. He couldn't hide his frozen tears and looked away while he spoke. 'Will the police continue to work with the LandSAR team and look elsewhere? What's their plan?'

She searched his face and then Elly's—sensitive that they desperately wanted answers like she did.

Her voice also began to quaver. 'I don't know if they'll continue the search—at least, not here in Piha. They may start looking in the rest of the Waitakere Ranges, but it's such an expansive area and I don't see how they can know where to look. They have no concrete evidence she even disappeared from here.'

There were a few moments of silence again.

Peter leapt to his feet. 'Sorry, I've got to get off home now. I've got a few things to do before I hit the hay. Thanks, both of you.'

Briar stayed to chat with Elly, while Peter trudged aimlessly home. He was at an all-time low. He had placed his faith and trust in God, but it didn't seem to stop his anxiety when his imagination ran wild. Al knew a lot more than he was letting on and Peter was determined to get at the truth.

Chapter Ten

Peter opened his fridge and pulled out a bowl of leftovers—his favourite salad with shredded chicken marinated in honey and sesame soy sauce. Sandy had once taken pity of him living alone without a clue how to prepare a decent meal for himself. With her help, he had progressed from living on takeaways to creating nutritional, gourmet delights. Through her encouragement, he had become a decent chef.

On hot summer days, a plate of salad was all he could stomach while dealing with the anxiety and grief caused by Sandy's disappearance.

He finished his meal, glanced at the wall clock and decided it was time to phone Al. He breathed a sigh of relief when the Detective Inspector answered the phone immediately, as most evenings Peter found him hard to pin down. When Al answered, he plugged him for information about the body washed up on Keyhole Rock.

'I don't think you understand, Peter—I can't discuss evidence found at a crime scene. You'll just have to keep your ear close to the ground and listen to the radio and TV news releases. There should be one tonight, and once it has been released to the public, I can talk to you about it.'

'I just need to know if you've identified that chap who Sandy was worried about from the rehab centre.'

'Yes—we've identified him and we're trying to locate him to bring him in for questioning.'

Peter's heart somersaulted into his throat.

'Well, surely you can tell me if you know if he is associated with the man who was washed up on the beach—even if you can't tell me his name.'

'No, I can't do that! Look ... these things take time ... I mean forensics, and I'm sure you would want us to be thorough and not miss anything. I can assure you—as soon as I can release information, you will be the first to know.'

After Peter had hung up the phone, he felt a degree of comfort that this detective would be considerate enough to let him know their findings first, rather than having to wait until he heard it on the news. He guessed that Al believed that he was innocent although he couldn't let him off the hook in case he was implicated in something sinister regarding Sandy.

Only one more day of searching the Piha area before the police would begin focusing their attention in other parts of the Waitakere Ranges. But the bush was so expansive it would be like finding a needle in a haystack. Perhaps she had tried a different track to one she already knew, and there were many popular walking tracks in the area—that's if she did go walking that day.

When Peter was stressed, he would head for the fridge and serve himself a heap of his favourite ice cream and then try to kid himself that his daily walks up Lion Rock would whittle the calories away.

At 6 pm the news came on the TV and once again, Sandy's disappearance was in the headline news.

"The body found at Keyhole Rock with injuries to the head has been identified as Manuel Santos, a New Zealand born Brazilian who was an experienced commercial diver."

He began to doze off and woke with a start—it was dark outside. He lurched at the windows to shut out the sand flies and mosquitoes that had started attacking him and began thinking about what he had heard on the news. He pondered the possibility that Sandy was kidnapped and it had gone wrong. Manuel Santos could well have been involved, as his body turned up soon after Sandy went missing.

His mind boggled as he glanced at his wristwatch and saw how late it was. He was suffered from brain drain and desperately needed sleep but doubted if he could switch off.

He drank a cup of camomile tea and honey which usually worked and lay on his bed. Sleep captured him quickly.

🐈 🐈 🐈

The sun streaming through Peter's linen curtains woke him early the next morning. Daylight saving annoyed him as the morning sunlight was bright in Piha and he kept telling himself to buy darker curtains and had never got around to it.

After gulping down a mug of coffee and scoffing toast and marmalade, he picked up the phone.

'Ah, here it is, *Living Free*. That's the name of the rehab centre Sandy told us about,'

77

he mumbled to himself, as he surfed the net on his mobile phone.

He rang the number he found on the internet and a receptionist answered.

'I am trying to locate someone who has recently been in your treatment centre. He wears his hair in dreadlocks and has a chain tattoo around his neck.'

'I'm sorry. I can't give out information about any of our clients unless you are the police—anyway—the tattoo probably fits the description of half of our clients here,' she said curtly. 'The dreads are a little different,' she added.

'No, I'm not the police,' he snapped. 'So do you know who I'm talking about? I just want to know if he had been at your centre in the last few months. That's all.'

'Yes he had—but he discharged himself and didn't complete his program. There's no point knowing that now, is there?'

'Yes, there is. My girlfriend has gone missing and according to her, he had been stalking her after he left rehab.'

The woman on the phone began to stammer. 'Look—you need to discuss all this with the police—not me.'

Beads of sweat formed on his brow and dripped down onto his nose. 'That's why I rang you. The police are so slow and I decided to do a little of my own detective work—I'm desperate for some answers.'

'I'm so sorry I'm not much help. I'll have to answer another call now. The police have been talking with our director. I'm sure they'll get to the bottom of it. Thanks for calling.'

The receptionist hung up abruptly just as Peter had more questions, but part of him knew he was barking up the wrong tree, as the woman would have been bound by client confidentiality just as the police are. He couldn't wait to get hold of the girls to tell them his news. He must phone Al to tell him what he knows, that's for sure.

Chapter Eleven

Briar met with Peter and Elly at the Surf Club where they, including Sandy, had always got together for a meal on a Friday evening.

Peter was running late after dropping architectural plans off to a client on Scenic Drive and arrived panting after rushing through the door.

'Wow—you're looking harried,' Elly spouted. 'There's no rush—we're just relaxing with a beer. Can I order you one?' she asked, jumping out of her seat.

He slid into the chair next to Briar. 'It's okay, thanks. I'll order one with my meal.'

Elly leaned across the table, straining to hear their conversations against the noise in the bar.

'So—what's the latest update on Sandy?' he asked.

'Did you hear this morning's news? The body at Keyhole Rock was a Brazilian commercial diver, but police announced that their lines of investigation are focused on the possible connection between his death and the missing young woman, Sandy Barrett.'

Peter's melancholic demeanour dampened the rest of the evening as he placed crossed arms on the table and stared at the sea. *That's what Al couldn't tell me.*

Briar elbowed him. 'Come on, Peter—buck up. Where's your faith? Sandy needs us to stay strong. They haven't got any evidence of that and have only started that investigation. Knowing Sandy, she's lost in the bush up in the ranges somewhere. You know her—she always takes risks—an adrenaline junkie. Someone will find her, but I hope it will be soon.'

Elly could see the tramlines of worry etched in Peter's forehead. 'She always goes hiking well-prepared. As long as she has water, she can survive, and it has rained heavily in the last few days remember.'

'Yes, but what if she has been kidnapped and that Brazilian fellow was involved? I'm sick of waiting around not knowing anything. And Al, the DI said that Carl is in the clear as he has an alibi. That only leaves me as the last person to be seen with Sandy. I'm sure he still thinks I could be involved. I'm going to have to do my own investigations to get myself off the hook.'

Briar glanced at Elly rolling her eyes.

Elly placed her hand on his arm. 'There's no way they can pin this on you—look, tell me what you want to do and I'll try to help. We are all in this together.'

'Thanks, Elly. I'm going to see what I can find out about this Manuel Santos— what connections he has around here and why the murder happened near Keyhole Rock.'

Briar huffed. 'Don't you think you need to leave that to the police? They have sophisticated methods of investigating suspects—far more than you could even imagine.'

Peter quietly rebuffed Briar's well-intended comment.

'Why don't you drop around tomorrow before you start work? You're on the afternoon shift, aren't you,' he asked Elly.

'Sure, I'll drop around after I've had a bit of a sleep in.'

'Great—I'll try to dig something up before then.'

'Ah, food!' said Briar, as the waitress brought their meals.'

Elly stood up to assist her colleague.

'No, you stay there. It's your evening off, time to relax,' said the young woman glancing at Peter and winking at Elly as she handed the plates around and walked off.

The following morning Peter was up early not having slept much the previous night. He was weary, as he had walked Elly and Briar back to their respective abodes after dinner at the Surf Club, and afterwards stayed up half the night on the internet searching for a lead that might connect the dead man to Sandy.

His heart missed several beats as he glued his eyes to his computer screen. There it was spelt out before him in an old Australian tabloid—*Manuel Santos, a commercial diver was acquitted of his suspected role as a mule in South American drug trade, Sydney. It is believed Santos has connections with drug cartels but has no criminal record in this country.*

'That's it!' Peter held his cat on his lap while sitting at the computer and happily chatted away to it. 'He may be involved with that fellow, Kingi who was hanging around Sandy not long before she disappeared. What do you think, puss? Maybe I'm jumping to conclusions.'

Later that morning, Peter startled at the sound of someone banging on the door. He opened it to find Elly standing there.

'Sorry—I was in my office on my computer and couldn't hear you knock at first. Come on in.'

'Hope you don't mind me dropping by. Are you still working?'

'No, I'm doing some investigative research on that Santos bloke.'

'Great—have you found anything?'

'Yeah, this article about his dodgy past.'

She put on her reading glasses and craned her neck over his shoulder.

'Wow, that's informative. It freaks me out to think that he could be involved with a cartel,' she said, squinting her eyes to take a closer look. 'I need my computer glasses instead of these. It's a bit small—you'll have to tell me what it says.'

Peter read out the article while Elly looked on.

'It's an old article written ten years ago and says he was acquitted of all charges relating to drugs found concealed on an oil rig in Australia where he worked as an underwater welder.'

'Wow! What else does it say?'

Peter glared intensely at the screen.

'Listen to this—although he was acquitted, the police had concerns about his connections with the South American cartel which operated between Australia, New Zealand

and Colombia, although they found no evidence connecting him to any crime. For a while, he was under surveillance.'

'It's all a bit creepy, don't you think—that his death is now deemed suspicious?' Elly wrapped her arms around herself. 'It sends chills through me.'

Peter surfed the web again. 'There have been several drug busts in this neck of the woods lately. Maybe he was doing crime—and right on our doorstep. Jeepers—we don't want those South American drug cartels here.'

'I think we've got to make our own enquiries around here. First of all—what was he doing in the vicinity of Keyhole Rock? They didn't find a boat and there are no houses in Whites Beach or Anawhata Beach—or are there?'

'Hiking, swimming or fishing I guess,' said Peter. He handed her a bottle of Mac's Ginger Beer. 'I suppose all of those options are possible. I know of an old hut tucked amongst the kauri trees near the main track that leads to Whites Beach from Anawhata Road. I came across it once while hiking between and it looked lived in, although that day there was no one in sight. We could go and see if there's anyone there today and ask questions. They would have had a good view of Keyhole Rock from there.'

Elly popped the top off the bottle and guzzled a few mouthfuls then caught herself. 'Let's go for a hike over to Whites Beach tomorrow and see if there are any locals in the area who may have seen Manuel. I mean—if he was Brazilian, he would have had an accent.'

'Not particularly—he was New Zealand born,' said Peter. 'It's still possible, I suppose. I kept the photo of him that was in the newspaper and I don't know how the police obtained that photo or how they were able to identify him.' Peter passed her the bowl of crisps they had been sharing.

'Forensics, of course. They do that with DNA and teeth. He was born here so that wouldn't have been a problem.'

Peter took out a small diary from his pocket. 'I think I have an appointment later today.' He looked at it and nodded. 'Yep, but I have some free time tomorrow. I have a meeting with a client at 6 pm so as long as we're back for that.'

'Cool—I'll pack some lunch for us both. I have to be back by 5 pm for the evening shift. Will that give us enough time?' said Elly.

'It sure will as long as we leave early—on second thoughts—we should go by car to the end of Anawhata Road and walk down the track to the beach. We could meet some of the residents who live in the area and ask if they knew anything about Manuel. I'll take my car.'

'Great idea. Unless you want to go on the back of my scooter,' she chuckled.

'I'll come by your house around ten if that's okay. Don't forget to wear strong walking shoes. It's pretty rugged around there.'

Chapter Twelve

'Wait for me,' Peter yelled, stopping to take a breath before he shot after Elly who'd opened the car door and fled towards the track, her day pack bouncing on her back.

'Careful on this track—it's steep,' he said, pulling on her sleeve to slow her down. 'I slipped down here a few years ago.'

Elly slowed her pace. When they arrived below, they both looked surprised to see the beach was busy. A black-backed gull squawked loudly above them as if it was trying to protect her young hidden away in the tussock grass.

Elly pulled her cap on her head. 'We should have brought our swimming togs. It's going to be sweltering in this heat and we're so exposed.'

'No time for that. I'm going to talk to those people over there carrying the fishing rods. Coming?'

Peter rushed up to a man and a woman carrying fishing gear about to walk back up the track. They were in luck as the people they quizzed were residents who had lived in the area for twenty years.

'Wow—what a find! They almost know everyone around here,' Peter said, excitedly. 'I'm glad we can access the track from the road as they said. I think he said it was past the house with the iron gate opposite the farm and the entrance to the track will be sign-posted.'

Elly pulled out roll-on sunblock from her day pack and applied it to her arms. She handed it to Peter.

'No, thanks. I put some on before we left. I think the old fella they told us about may know things that most people around here don't. He has lived here for more than thirty years and I hear that he is harmless, but knows everything that goes on. Let's go.'

They got back into the car and drove a few kilometres along the road parking next to the iron gate leading to a private road which accessed the track to Whites Beach.

After finding the entrance to the track down a steep walkway, the path veered off as they stumbled along the goat track that was almost non-existent, overgrown by flax and long grass—obviously not a well-trodden path, Peter realised as he struggled along with Elly in tow.

'How much longer?' Elly whined, after a ten-minute walk, while Peter stopped to wait for her to catch up. 'If I'd known the track was this difficult, I wouldn't have come.'

'We have to veer off to the right here somewhere and further along the ridge we should see his property from the track. The guy said there's a pohutukawa tree at the bottom of his section and a derelict red shed,' said Peter, bending down to retie his bootlace. He stood up grabbing the map from his pocket. 'It's supposed to be here—look.'

'It should be behind that group of rimu trees, see there.' Elly glanced up to where he was pointing and yanked her pack off her back to take out her water bottle. 'This is thirsty work. I hope he'll be there—I need to rest.'

'Sorry—I didn't know the track would be this wild and overgrown. After we visit the old man, we can sit and rest where we can look at the view over Whites Beach.'

'Wait—look!' Elly pointed to a grey-faced petrel that looked like it was nesting near the Pohutukawa tree. They veered away from the bird, climbing the path to the hut at the top of the hill.

They both stared aghast as they approached the hermit's aged dwelling. Peter wondered how it could still be standing, but it had been built of kauri wood and made to last, although it looked rough. As they approached the abode, a hunched man in baggy khaki shorts and a black singlet appeared from behind a make-shift clothesline hanging his towels.

'Hey!' he yelled, startled as he turned around. 'What are you doing up here? Not causing trouble, I hope?' He picked up a large stick and stood back.

'No—sorry to startle you,' Elly called. 'We were hoping you might be able to help us.'

Peter pulled out his business card and driver's licence to identify himself and they both shook his hand and introduced themselves.

'Jock's the name, but I'm known around here as Spring-heeled Jack, except not to my face. I do plenty of hikes around here and yonder as far as South Piha.' He pulled two wooden chairs out from under the eaves. 'Sit yourselves down and tell me what brings you to this neck of the woods.'

Elly was relieved of the rest, as they both plonked themselves down on the heavy kauri seats.

'Have you heard that a young woman called Sandy Barrett has gone missing from Piha almost a week ago?'

Jock's friendly expression changed to disapproval.

'What's all this—are you a cop—you think I have something to do with it?'

'Oh, no—not at all. She is a friend of ours. We heard you have good knowledge of the area and everyone who comes and goes, and we're hoping you may have seen or heard something to do with that fellow who was washed up on Keyhole Rock the day after her disappearance. His name is Manuel Santos, a Brazilian guy. The police think he may be connected to Sandy going missing—a hostage situation or such like.'

Jock picked up the stick he'd dropped and started to scratch the dry ground with it.

Peter broke the silence. 'We're trying to work out why he was found in this area. His head had been bashed in, the police said. They didn't find a vehicle belonging to him so he must have been on a boat.'

'I know the one you're talking about. He comes here a few times a year. You know he owns a bach tucked away in the bush in Whites Beach? It's hidden from any of the walking tracks. I always thought it was a bit dodgy, but Sir Edmund Hillary had a bach for years in the bush in these parts too. Some folk, I included, like to get away from it all and enjoy the wilderness.'

Peter gave Elly a wry smile. She sat there taking it all in, not knowing what to say and let Peter do the talking.

'Would you like some fresh water? I've got plenty still.' Jock pointed to the large plastic drums next to his hut. 'It's filtered rainwater and cleaner than most of that city muck.'

'Thanks—my bottle needs filling, so I will,' said Peter.

Jock took his bottle and placed it under the tap on one of the drums. 'Won't do you any harm. I've been doing this for donkey's ages.' He handed it back. 'How about you miss?'

Elly handed him her bottle after unscrewing the lid.

'And I generate my power from that panel up there on the roof. Solar heating—it costs me nothing.'

'How do you get around? How about getting provisions?' Peter asked.

'In my Jeep out the back.'

Peter and Elly walked around the back of the hut and gaped in astonishment at the driveway that led onto Anawhata Road. They could have accessed Jock's property from there, had they known.

'Most of the time, I walk everywhere. That's why I'm called Spring-heeled Jack.'

'I reckon that guy who gave us the directions brought us deliberately on a wild goose chase when we could have driven here,' Peter whispered in Elly's ear.

They sat back down and listened to Jock excitedly tell about his self-sufficiency accomplishments. He even offered them a bowl of fresh raspberries he had grown himself. 'Help yourselves—sorry, no cream—the last cow died on me,' he said, bursting into laughter as his guests followed.

'I eat plenty of fish and sometimes swap them with a side of lamb or a chicken from the local farmer. I'm all set up here with solar power for heating and gas for hot water and cooking and I'm on a septic tank.'

Peter began to get restless, scuffing his boots under his chair. 'Can you tell us any more about this Brazilian fellow?'

Jock's eyes narrowed. He hesitated, looked them both over and opened up.

'There is one thing that didn't add up last summer. I was walking down to Whites Beach to take my daily swim which I do during the summer months, as it doesn't get dark until nine. That day it was late afternoon just before the sun went down, and one of those inflatable boats turned up. Two blokes were at the helm and one of them jumped out and met Santos, handing him a black bag while the other stayed at the wheel. As soon as he took the bag, the two sped off, quick as lightning. Santos scurried up the track to his bach, faster than I've seen him walking before. I stayed hidden behind a tea tree.'

'Why did you hide—did you suspect him of something?' Elly asked.

'Just in case he was doing something illegal. I didn't want to get involved.'

'That's interesting what you told us. Maybe he was up to no good,' said Peter.

Jock stood up with his hands on his hips. 'Look—don't go quoting me on that—there could have been anything in that bag. It's just the way he grabbed it from them and took off fast as lightning.'

Peter and Elly stood up, grasping the hint that it was time to move on.

Jock lifted his straw sunhat off to scratch his head and replaced it. 'Did you know his family live in Australia and he has a brother there he stays with when he is over there?'

'Goodness, Jock—you seem to be a resource for a vast amount of information. How is it that you know so much?' Peter asked with a quizzical expression on his face.

'Because I too made several enquiries about him several years ago when I accidentally stumbled upon his new bach after it had been built. I had been staying down south house-sitting my sister's dogs while she and her husband were on an overseas trip for a few months. When I was out walking a short time after I returned, I was surprised to see another dwelling had arrived in the area.'

Peter shot Elly a glance, raising his eyebrows and said to Jock, 'Well—this is all a huge advancement on what information we've had. I'd be interested to find out if the police know his history—I guess they do.'

'Don't go giving them my details, but any time you want to know anything, just come to old Jock. They call me the town crier in these parts,' he said, with a broad, toothy smile.

'Thanks for everything, Jock,' said Peter, shaking his hand. 'You've been a great help. Here's my phone number.' Peter handed him a business card. 'Drop by sometime for a visit at Piha.'

'That's mighty good of you. I have a mobile phone but can't get reception. I have to get onto Anawhata Road to pick up anything. There's better reception out at sea, would you believe?'

'Well—you can always drop by any time. My address is on the card—I work from home.'

'Where are you parked—up the top? I didn't hear your vehicle.'

'Nope, we didn't know you had access from the road and we're parked way along Anawhata Road before the access to the farm walk.'

'Let me drive you there,' said Jock, rattling his keys in his pocket.

'No, thanks mate. We want to check out Santos's place and see if we can find out anything else. But if you don't mind, we'll access the road afterwards from your driveway.'

'No problem—you'd better be careful after what you told me. I wouldn't hang around his place for long.'

Elly tugged the sleeve of Peter's anorak. 'We should get going, sorry—I've got to be back in time for work.'

Peter made a move. 'Thanks, again Jock—I also need to get a move on. I have a meeting with a client. Bye for now.'

'Wait, a minute, I think I can do something to help—stay here.' Jock scuttled inside the hut and returned with a pen and paper. 'I'm going to draw a little map to show you how to find that fellow's bach. It's not too far from here, but it's easy to lose the track, as it's pretty overgrown.'

Jock's gnarled, sun-tanned fingers made a quick sketch of the area, pinpointing the bach then stood waving them both off as they headed down the track.

Chapter Thirteen

When they arrived at the top of the hilly track overlooking Whites Beach, unbeknown to them, Sandy lay nearby, injured. Elly plonked herself down on a patch of flat ground covered with brown grass, looking out at the spectacular view as they tried to piece together all that Jock had told them.

'We have to investigate this Santos fellow and try to look inside his place. He's hardly going to turn up and catch us now, is he? It's a wonder the police don't know about his bach.'

Peter took another few mouthfuls of water and rummaged in his day pack. 'Ah, here it is—my muesli bar. Would you like one?' he asked, handing a packet to Elly.

'No thanks, I've packed plenty of food. I'd rather wait until we stop for a bite. We are, aren't we?'

Peter tore open the snack bar and stuffed the empty packet into his day pack. 'Yep,' he said, chomping on the snack. 'How about stopping for lunch after we take a look at that fellow's bach? We'd better head back after that. We could walk back to the car along the side of the road. It will be a lot easier.'

Elly hauled herself up off the ground. 'Sounds like a great idea—let's go!'

'I think Al may be right in thinking that Manuel was involved in some kind of criminal activity that back-fired on him—but I don't think it was a kidnapping. My guess is he was moving illicit items, be it drugs or laundered money—may be involved with a gang or an international cartel.'

'What?' Elly's mouth fell wide open, matching her goggle eyes. 'Really—could that be possible?'

Peter got up and followed her traipsing down the grassy path surrounded by a thick carpet of bracken ferns and tea tree. 'Yep absolutely—wide-scale operations are being undertaken by our drug squads to combat international drug syndicates smuggling huge quantities of cocaine into New Zealand and Australia right now. The problem has reached mammoth proportions.'

'Oh, my goodness, I had no idea—in New Zealand too? It sounds horrible,' Elly said, shuddering suddenly.

'Ow—darn thing!' Peter stumbled on a tree root on the path. He waited until he found his balance and they continued along the track.

'So, with that in mind, I hate to say it but Santos may be involved in a major drug run and it appears more likely that Sandy wasn't kidnapped,' he said, arriving at a small, compact building set in a glade of kauri trees, just as Jock had described.

'Wait here,' Peter said quietly to Elly as she stayed behind a tree. 'I'll make sure there's no one here first. It could be dangerous.'

Peter crept over to the bach crouching as he approached a window. Most of the curtains were drawn, but there was one window where the curtains weren't properly closed. He carefully edged his way peering through the window. He beckoned Elly to wait and crept around the outside of the building and then returned, waving at her to join him.

'No sign of anyone, thank God. I'd love to take a look inside but that would be too risky in case one of his thug mates arrives.'

'Look—it appears lived in and there are breakfast items on the dining table as though he left in a hurry one morning and hasn't returned since,' said Peter, pushing his face against the window.

They took one last look and moved on. 'Let's clear out of here,' said Peter. 'I'm not keen on coming head to head with a Brazilian cartel or the likes.'

'What shall we do with all this information we've gathered—do you think that the police know all this?' Elly asked, following him back along the track from where they'd come from.

'I'm not sure. They may not know about the bach in the bush, as he doesn't stay there often. But I'm sure going to phone Al when we get back and make a time to see him—the sooner the better, as Sandy could still have been implicated somehow.'

They trudged back up towards Jock's place and before they accessed the road from his driveway, they stopped for lunch where they could sit and enjoy the spectacular view of the ocean, overlooking Whites Beach and Anawhata Beach.

The rest of the time they spent eating their late lunch, they were both deep in thought, trying to piece it all together. Peter was overwhelmed by all the new information they had received from Jock. After a short time, he looked at his watch and realised they would have to make tracks back to his vehicle to get Elly to work on time. It had been a day well spent in his mind.

Although jubilant at the breakthrough they'd received from Jock, Peter still needed to prove his own innocence and was not out of the woods yet, being the last person to be seen with Sandy before she vanished. Even if the police discovered that the death of Santos was drug-related, and it had no connection to Sandy whatsoever—what then? It was a mystery and he mustn't give up the search.

Please God, help me find a way through this insurmountable mountain.

Chapter Fourteen

'Hi Peter,' said Al, over the cell phone, 'How about I meet you at your house at 4 pm tomorrow. While this case is running, I'll be working from the Piha Police Station next to Barnett Hall.'

'Thanks, Al I appreciate you coming so promptly. Maybe urgency is what is needed right now. I'll see you then.'

Peter was mentally exhausted. He had dropped Elly off home and met up with a client straight after. Following the phone call, he was depleted. Meeting Jock and taking everything in that he had learnt from the recluse had drained him. He began feeling the strain of losing his best friend and hoped that the waiting would soon be over.

DI Crawford sat at his desk swilling his near cold mug of coffee and eating a tuna wrap while perusing the coroner's report and an investigation summary from the Criminal Investigation Branch that his colleague, Ben Crosby had handed him.

The forensic report stated that Manuel had died from a severe blow to the back of the head. Al raised grimaced. It detailed how his body must have been dumped into the sea after he was dead, and the injury to the back of his skull had resulted in a compressed fracture.

There were some suggestions from the CIB that gangs could be involved—a misadventure gone wrong and that he had links with international organised crime. Ben watched Al's face as he read the report and waited, but no response.

Ben was determined to find a clue somehow, and the local people would help him, he was sure. With a Brazilian name like Manuel Santos, the victim was bound to have had connections with the South American community.

Al sat picking his teeth with a toothpick he took from his pocket. 'Looks like this Santos fellow has got himself into trouble with gang members, but we've no proof, of course.'

Ben pondered on whether Santos could be involved with a drug cartel called the Poderosa he had been researching. But this guy was New Zealand born and his family lived in Australia. That wouldn't make sense—or would it? He couldn't understand why Al huffed at Ben's original suggestion of Santos being tied up with a cartel.

The police team were increasingly alarmed by the number of drug cartels entering New Zealand and Australia, that fact Ben did know, as they had employed more staff to combat the problem. They had to find the drug barons who worked with stealth and were difficult to track with false identities. But this time, he just had to concentrate his efforts on finding the young woman missing from Piha and to see if her disappearance was linked to the murder of Santos.

Ben took a phone call in his office. When he finished, he knocked on Al's door.

'Sir—you won't believe this and it could be a hoax like the others we've had when people have gone missing on West Auckland beaches. Our anonymous tip line received a call regarding the death of Santos. The caller said he saw an SOS signal coming from the vicinity of Whites Beach near the lookout the night before Santos was found at Keyhole Rock. He said he knows that the assault was carried out by the cartel called the Poderosa, one of the most ruthless drug cartels in Columbia.'

Al scowled at him. 'Give me the report,' he snapped.

Crosby sneezed into his handkerchief as he handed Al the informer's telephone report.

A large cocaine haul has been smuggled by a cartel onto a New Zealand super Yacht called Toledo from the Far North which is now moored in the Bay of Islands and ready to cast off tomorrow. The drugs have been transported by a mother ship which met up with the yacht in the Pacific and stored the drugs in the rudder compartments of the ships. The informer stated he wanted to leave the cartel but was forced to dive for the cocaine on the yacht against his will. His drug boss had threatened to harm his family if he didn't play ball, as he claimed that he owed him, which was untrue. He said he was concerned that the girl missing from Piha may have sent the SOS and could die. His boss told him to deal with whoever sent the message, as they would have witnessed the killing, but he couldn't go through with harming her. If it was the woman who was missing, he said he knows her personally. She helped him and his family once and wanted to repay her by sparing her life. He wouldn't say how he knows her. He said he could give names and addresses and blow this whole operation apart.

Crosby stood waiting to hear Al comment on the report, who was apathetic.

'Do you think it's a hoax?' Ben asked, leaning against the doorpost.

'I'm not sure,' Al retorted. 'You'd better get onto the tech team to try and trace the call.'

'The tech team have checked. He used an untraceable burner phone, but they are checking voice detection. Shouldn't we contact LandSAR?' he asked, wide-eyed.

'I guess we'll have to, but I hope it's not a hoax as we've had a lot of people looking up there already. We'll check it out first and then go from there. I'll contact the marine police and get that yacht examined. The owner has probably fled the country already.'

Crosby interjected. 'But it had rained heavily the day before they went in, and her tracks would have been washed away. The narrow path through the bush is caked with mud up there. One of the rescue team said the track was barely recognisable after that flash flood so that could still have been her sending an SOS.'

'The team have been back since and had dogs in the bush. If she was anywhere near, they'd have found her,' answered Al in an irritated tone.

Crosby's mood sank. 'I hope it's not a hoax call.'

'It's possible,' said Al. 'Plenty of people holding a grudge against coppers will do anything to burden us with unnecessary work and send us on a wild goose chase.'

'There's also a slim chance he knows her. Let's hope she is still alive and can shed some light on this if she is found in time,' Crosby replied. 'I'll see what I can find on the internet too. I'm off on a lunch break now, if that's okay.'

Al stretched his arms clasping his hands. 'It's alright for some. I've been up half the night with this business. I'll phone if I need you, but don't go far. In the meantime, I'll organise a small search party to head up to the lookout above White Beach to have a look around. When you get back from lunch, you had better alert the Marine Police about that yacht, before it disappears from here.'

Crosby frowned and slipped away to lunch before he could change his mind. Al worked his team hard but always got results and couldn't afford to lose control of his staff. Signs were showing of his unhealthy attachment to his job since his wife had left, accusing him of being a workaholic. Grey hair had appeared prematurely at forty-five and crow's feet gathered around the corners of his eyes. Deep dark trenches etched under his intense blue eyes had aged him.

Compulsively running his finger along a thick scar on his chin, he picked up the coroner's report and re-read it then got up, placed it on Ben's desk for filing and returned to his computer.

Al stayed glued to the screen waiting for Ben's return until he remembered to cancel his meeting with Peter and called to tell about the new search for Sandy.

It would be a race against time to find Sandy Barrett if she was still alive—especially if she was a key witness to any activities of the Poderosa cartel. Crosby was desperate to discover what she saw from her vantage point on the side of the cliff.

The LandSAR were on the ball by midday with the search party and police dogs scanning the bush at the top of the cliffs by the lookout with another team on the beach below. The rescue helicopter hovered above, but visibility was difficult due to the towering pohutukawa trees and dense bush. They continued the search until the sun went down at nine. Their efforts were futile, but unbeknown to them, fifty metres down the steep rocky cliff tucked away in a small cleft lay a young woman subconsciously clutching onto life with every last breath she took.

The search was over and while Al and Crosby drove back to the station after supervising the search, a feeling of deflation weighed heavily on Crosby's soul.

'Perhaps it was a prank,' Al murmured out the side of his mouth to Crosby as they drove back to the office. 'This is the last time we conduct a search for her up there—it's a waste of manpower. Sounds like this fellow had it in for his drug boss and used Sandy as justification to call us and dob in his drug smuggling mate.'

'It sure sounds like, it,' said Crosby. But I do think we'd better take his confession about the yacht moored in Paihia in the Bay of Islands seriously. The drug squad have been trying to track down these cartels smuggling drugs into New Zealand from South America for years,' he said, pulling out a packet of sugar-free gum and popping one into his mouth.

Al nodded and shrugged, showing he had little energy for the task at hand, happy to let his younger colleague expend his energy in solving the case.

'New Zealand customs have been working with coast guards and police in Australia and the Pacific and had certain ships under surveillance waiting for the right time to

pounce. Maybe this is it. I'll get right onto it in
the morning,' said Crosby.

Chapter Fifteen

Sandy's pain had faded into insignificance so that she felt euphoric. He legs felt numb after lying in one position for so long. Perhaps she was in heaven already or she'd lapsed into some sort of coma. Huddled in a heap clutching her half-empty water bottle, she drifted into oblivion once again.

The sensation of something soft pushing against her cheek startled her back to reality. She felt it again, and this time it deposited moisture on her face, making her cringe. Was it some strange creature that had come to consume her? As far as she was aware, there were no such things in caves in New Zealand.

Then she heard a whimpering sound like a baby whining. Whatever it was, it nudged her arm. She took a deep breath, and with all her might opened her eyes and raised her hand to touch whatever it was that gently pushed her arm. Instantly it dawned on her as large tears stung her dry eyes. 'Sleuth, my darling! Oh, my dear Sleuth—you've come to save me. Thank you, God!' His soft nose nuzzled into her neck and he licked her continuously. In the muted light of early dawn dancing on the cave walls, she could see his tail wagging with fury.

'Oh God—you sent me a rescuer—thank you!'

She took a few mouthfuls of water. It had been a week since she'd left home and her food had gone. She knew that she wouldn't last long without water unless it rained again and had conserved it.

The dog snuggled into her side, resting his head on her chest. A few hours later, she woke and realised she had to do something, her last chance of a rescue.

From oblivion to extreme pain, she rolled on her side to try to reach the stick she had used as a flag with her red crop bra tied to it and painstakingly eased the knot open. Next, she unclipped the gold chain from around her neck baring a gold crucifix that Peter had once given her. Taking hold of Sleuth's collar, she secured the rolled-up garment to the collar and then wound the chain around it, fastening the clip so that it would show up against the red background.

'Go, boy—get help. Go home—get Briar. Off you go home, boy!'

Sleuth peered at her with sad, puppy-dog eyes and whimpered. He licked her hand and lifted his paw, placing it on her arm. He whined again and as Sandy collapsed in a debilitated heap, laid his head on her chest, waiting for her to become responsive again. When he could see that she appeared to be sleeping, he took off up through the bush at the side of the cave, scaling the sheer bank he had just slid down to get to Sandy and ran off down the track to Piha.

🐕 🐕 🐕

Something woke him, or was he still dreaming? Peter pulled the sheet over his head to block out the light zeroing in on him from the early morning sun. The clamour was persistent, and then he realised it was a familiar sound. His cell phone was ringing, blaring his favourite melody causing him to startle and jump out of bed to answer it. He knocked it flying off the dresser in his haste, grateful to see it land on his bed. The caller had rung off.

He cupped his head in his hands. 'What a way to start the day with a blinking headache—stress, probably,' he muttered to himself. Checking his caller ID he rang Briar.

115

'Hi, there—you called. Sorry, but I sent my phone flying trying to answer it. I slept in after a heavy day yesterday.'

'No worries—I guess you're feeling the same as I am. But something else has cropped up. Sleuth ran away early this morning after I took him for a brief walk around six. Before I could lock the gate he shot off. He has done this a few times in the past when there was a dog on heat nearby, but not since. He always returned home by the end of the day. I have to get to work and don't know what to do.'

'Oh, bother! I've got a deadline this morning with a plan for a client, I can look for him this afternoon..'

'Thanks, Peter. Elly's at work already and they have a birthday luncheon to host, so she can't take time off. I'll give you a call later.'

'Wait—I guess you haven't heard that the LandSAR completed another full-scale search for Sandy yesterday afternoon around the lookout but found nothing. Apparently, they had a tip-off which Al said must have been a hoax.'

'Oh—that's pretty upsetting to hear, Peter. I hate to think what could have happened to her. We just have to have faith and stay strong.'

His day was ruined. He'd hoped to be able to have time out from all the stress, but he couldn't sit back and let Sandy's beloved pet go astray. He prayed for Sleuth's protection and trusted Briar's confidence that the animal would return home by the end of the day.

He finished his meeting with his client earlier than he expected and changed into beach shorts and walking shoes ready to start looking for Sleuth.

'As if I haven't got enough going on without having to spend the day looking for a dog,' he muttered to himself. He went back into the kitchen to drink the remains of the coffee in his mug and felt someone was standing behind him. As he looked around at the open door, something rushed at him almost knocking him over.

'Sleuth! What the ... come here you great fluff ball. Where did you get to all this time?' He leaned over and while the dog licked him half to death, he grabbed the regalia from around his neck. A tight knot formed in his throat as stomach acid drowned his tonsils. 'Well, if this isn't the strangest thing,' he said, frantically undoing the garment on his collar until a red crop bra dropped on the floor revealing a gold chain and crucifix fastened to the dog's neck. His hands shook so much his fingers struggled to grasp the fastener to undo it as he recognised the crucifix. Beads of perspiration formed on his forehead until the necklace dropped into the palm of his hand. Surely his eyes deceived him. He sat down, cherishing his find and phoned Briar's cell phone in a panic.

'Please come around here quickly after you finish work. Sleuth has turned up and I think he can tell us where Sandy is.'

Briar told him she was able to finish work early and be there in thirty minutes.

When she arrived in Peter's lounge, he handed her the items to examine. Her face dropped as she recognised them straight away.

'The red crop bra … it's Sandy's! I know because I often do her washing with mine and hang it out. I know it in every detail as we both bought one at a sportswear closing down sale. I wear mine at Pilate classes with red leggings.'

In the bright sunlight, Peter could see tramlines of worry etched in her temples. He blushed and turned away at the talk about women's underwear while she continued. 'And the crucifix—that's the one you gave her, isn't it?'

'It is for sure. And Sleuth is going to take us to her, aren't you, boy?' He handed him a dog biscuit from an ice cream container that he kept whenever he had a visit from the dog. 'It's your reward for helping me find Sandy.'

Peter put the kettle on. 'Coffee or tea?'

'Yes, I'd love a coffee if that's okay.' She slumped into one of his armchairs. 'Where do we go from here—do you think Sleuth is going to lead us to her? Shouldn't we contact Al or the LandSAR first?'

Peter flicked his wrist to glance at his watch. 'No, not yet. I think we should take Sleuth out on a reconnaissance walk to see where he leads us. He knows you and me and he may not cooperate with the police and LandSAR. We can tell them after we know what's going on.'

While Briar sat drinking her coffee, tears welled up in her dark brown eyes. 'Let's hope this is the breakthrough we've been waiting for.'

Within minutes, Peter bounded back into the lounge. 'We don't know what we're going to find, Briar, so be prepared for the best or the worst.'

A chill tore through him as he fought uninvited thoughts of what fate may have befallen her.

'I changed into my walking boots. I see you're wearing yours—that's good.'

🐾 🐾 🐾

Deep in oblivion, Sandy dreamed she heard a dog crying. It must be in pain. Where is it? Her eyelids wouldn't open and her legs felt heavy. Her lucid intervals were few and far between and this time she vaguely remembered something nudging her, and what felt like a wet tongue against her cheek. It must be Sleuth. 'Are you still there, boy? Help me, please—you've got to help me, boy.' Her breath expired until she went flat again. Weakness had overtaken her and Sleuth had gone.

Chapter Sixteen

Peter strained to keep hold of the muscle-bound Retriever as he lurched forward out of Briar's gate and down onto the dunes digging his front paws into the sand trying to bolt.

'We'll stay behind him to see which direction he's headed first,' said Peter to Briar who stayed close behind.

'Hey, easy does it, boy. I know you think you're a tracker dog, but I'm not letting you go.'

Sleuth appeared to be pulling him in the direction of North Piha. 'Mmm, just as I thought—his favourite spot, it seems. He has run away up this way a few times when I let him off the lead.'

When they arrived at North Piha at the base of the steps leading up Whites track, Peter stopped. Sleuth tugged hard on his lead and whimpered loudly and then began to bark. 'See what I mean?' It dawned on Peter why the dog had wanted him to go up Whites track each time he took him for a walk.

When they reached the top of the track Sleuth led them to the lookout over Whites Beach. He became more agitated and almost toppled Peter down the bank leading to the towering cliffs overlooking the beach from the lookout.

'Hey, wait, boy!' Peter yelled, unnerved. He turned to Briar who had been in close pursuit.

'What shall I do? He wants to go down that cliff face covered with thick undergrowth, and I'm afraid to let him go.'

Briar walked closer to the edge where it began to drop away while Sleuth pulled Peter sideways trying to head off into the dense bush. 'Careful—you wouldn't want to fall down there. It's the same height as Lion Rock—a hundred metres to the bottom.'

Peter began calling Sandy's name repeatedly. Suddenly he unclipped Sleuth's lead, and the dog bolted fast as lightning into the bush leading to the side of the cliff.

'Hey! What did you do that for? You don't know that she's down there and it's not safe for him,' cautioned Briar.

'She's there, alright—I've no doubt now and Sleuth is a sure-footed Retriever. He wants to rescue her.'

'Well, if she is, we'll need LandSAR to bring climbing gear. They are on standby, so I think you should alert them now.'

🐾 🐾 🐾

Peter sat on the stone seat at the lookout and waited, while Briar stood scuffing her shoes, not knowing how to help until the silence was interrupted by a dog howling. After a short time, they heard the long flax leaves rustling and saw a clump of giant tussock grass moving. Suddenly Sleuth's welcome head popped up.

'Look, it's Sleuth—and he's got something in his mouth.' Peter walked towards the dog who bounded up to him, dropping a shoe he held in his mouth.

'Good boy,' he said patting him and picking up the shoe.

'Unbelievable—this is Sandy's—one of her new Kathmandu tramping shoes. She's down there!' Briar blurted.

Peter grabbed hold of Sleuth and clipped his lead back on. 'Come on—we have to get back and phone Al. Can you get any coverage on your phone? If so, I'd like to ring him, thanks. They'll have to get climbers and a helicopter up here.'

As they arrived at the bottom of the steps and tore across the black sand, Briar rushed at Peter in tears, wrapping her arms around him. 'Oh, thank God you didn't give up, Peter. I can't believe she is here somewhere.' He turned around to reveal red eyes and wet cheeks. Traipsing across the sand they were able to get cell phone reception. Peter phoned Al to organise a rescue and when he clicked off the phone, his heart bubbled over with joy at the miraculous breakthrough.

Al eventually arrived with Crosby and occupied himself setting up his high-frequency radio, ready for communications with LandSAR at the lookout, and if necessary, the rescue helicopter.

He came off the HF radio and grabbed Peter's attention. 'Two abseilers are on their way. If they can't get her out, the helicopter will. We'll just have to stand back and let them do their job.'

'I'm an experienced canyoner and abseiler with the West Auckland Canyoning Club—I can help too. Please let me go down with the other rescuer.'

'Ah—I don't think that would be appropriate seeing you are still under surveillance.'

'What?' Peter bawled. 'I want to save her not harm her!'

The two detectives sat on the stone seat that looked out over Whites Beach while Peter stood next to them.

'You don't know how important it is for me to go into that cave. I know she is alive and I want my face to be the first she sees.'

Peter failed to be able to tell them that Sandy was secretly the love of his life, although she didn't know, and these men would just laugh at that sentiment.

A sick feeling came over him as adrenaline surged through his veins. *What if they find her dead? I don't think I could cope— not after all this. Please God, please let her be alive.*

🐈 🐈 🐈

Within a short time, two men arrived with their abseiling gear. One of them stayed up top while his partner, a paramedic shimmied down the gap which was closed in by thick bush and pohutukawa trees to a ledge and cave that were partially hidden by tea tree that had been identified by the rescue helicopter.

The paramedic managed to find his way into the cave. Within minutes, the climber waiting above felt the tug on his rope which was a signal Sandy was there. The rescuer below carried a mountain radio that communicated with his climbing partner and the rescue helicopter.

'It's Sandy—she's alive!' he shouted to the detectives, while Peter's legs buckled causing him to collapse back onto the stone seat. 'Thank you!' he burst forth loudly.

Crosby patted him on the back. 'You are most definitely off the hook now. I'm sorry for what we put you through, but you can see it from our point of view that everyone becomes a suspect.'

'Yeah, I know,' he murmured, his voice shaking as much as his legs.

'Now let's get her out of here fast,' said Al.

The helicopter lowered a stretcher to the rescuer who went back into the cave to fetch Sandy. Although he was a trained paramedic, he still required instructions from the doctor on the helicopter by radio.

'It's going to be difficult to get the stretcher up on the cable, as the trees and bush hinder the pilot's visibility. There's a strong southerly breeze coming off the sea,' said the climber who stood talking to Al, waiting to see if he needed to go down to help.

'You may need another rescuer to assist if you're going to bring her up manually,' said Al.

Peter became anxious pacing up and down, now and then peering over the edge of the lookout to see if he could catch a glimpse of Sandy.

The paramedic dragged the stretcher with the victim out into the opening of the cave. Semi-conscious, she turned her head to shield her eyes from the glare while they waited for the pilot to approach close enough to be able to hoist up the stretcher.

The climber standing at the top listened to the rescuer's voice through his headphone. 'Sorry, Jerry. I'm not going to be able to get that stretcher up there safely. It's going to spin and there's no room to get in close. I'll need help down here to bring her down onto the beach instead.'

The climber repeated the message to Al who turned to Peter. 'They are going to take her down in the stretcher to the beach and will need more help. I'll contact LandSAR to send another climber. They're on standby.'

'No—wait! I'll go down—I'm an experienced climber with rescue experience—let me, please.'

Al was taken aback at his expression of desperation.

'This is no place for heroics, mate, no matter how much you like the girl,' he said with a wry smile. 'I suppose now that we know there's been no foul play, and she's alive—you could be an extra pair of hands. I'll still need to call for backup assistance. You already saved her life by being so persistent and following her dog.'

Before Al finished his sentence, Peter rushed off to speak with Jerry who was busy unpacking extra ropes from his backpack.

Peter burst forth with a barrage of how he had the go-ahead from Al to assist and gave a quick exposé of his expertise in climbing and abseiling. Jerry checked with Al first.

'Okay—throw this gear on and listen to every word I say,' Jerry said, unravelling a pile of safety clothing from his kit he'd left under a tree. 'I'll let my partner know down below.'

Peter's face said it all, brimming from ear to ear. While Briar sat on the stone seat out of the way, Peter pulled the thick pants over his shorts, fastened the rescuer's jacket and donned climbing gloves. Picking up the safety helmet off the ground, he first walked over to Briar.

'Sorry—I kind of feel I'm leaving you out of all this, but I just want to get down to her—you understand—I know you do.'

'Get on down there—I know how important she is to you—no point hiding it anymore,' she said with a half-smile.

Al didn't have time to summon another. Jerry had tied a couple of ropes to the trunk of a huge rimu tree and after he'd rigged up his belay system, he began lowering Peter as he abseiled down to the rescuer below.

No sooner than he landed on his feet on the ledge, Peter bent over the stretcher and prodded Sandy. 'It's Peter, Sandy, wake up!'

She made no response. 'Is she okay—have you checked her neurological status?'

'Yes, she's going to be okay. She's dehydrated and has fractures, but once we get her onto the beach, I'll give her intravenous fluids. The chopper will take her from there.'

Peter leaned over her again. 'Sandy, it's me—Peter. Open your eyes—let me know you're okay.' He wanted to take her hand, but she had been enclosed safely in the stretcher.

His heart sank as she lay there listless and unresponsive—and then a smile. Although a faint one, it was enough to still Peter's nerves and her eyes smiled too.

'Oh, thank God, you're still with us. Please hang in there. You'll soon be in a comfortable hospital bed and I'll be there with you soon.'

'Okay, mate—time to move. My name is Tom, by the way. Jerry is on his way down to help us. I'll belay you to the beach below and we'll bring her down in the stretcher—we're used to this.'

Once on the beach, Peter waited for Tom to join him then they operated the ropes below while Jerry walked down the cliff face with Sandy fastened tightly in the stretcher. Once they stabilised her, they loaded her into the chopper which had landed on Whites Beach on the hard sand.

'Hey, mate. You can come on board if you want to accompany her to the hospital. It's up to you,' said Tom.

Without a moment's hesitation, he climbed in and gave thanks again to his creator for saving her life. Until this day, he hadn't realised how much she meant to him, that she was more than just a friend, in his eyes.

Chapter Seventeen

Al offered Briar and Sleuth a ride home in his vehicle with Crosby.

'Well—that was a hair-raising experience. I can't believe Sleuth found her,' said Briar with an emotional tremble in his voice.

Al fastened his seatbelt and looked over his shoulder at the notorious dog who lay his head on Briar's lap.

'You and Peter had your part to play in her rescue. If you both hadn't responded to Sleuth the way you did, I don't think she would be alive much longer. According to the paramedic, she wouldn't have lasted more than a few days as her water bottle was empty,' said Crosby with a warm smile.

Briar shuddered at his words and cuddled Sleuth all the way home while Al said very little.

🐾 🐾 🐾

That evening, the rescue was all over the news. Tearful, Briar phoned Elly to tell her the breath-taking experience she had watched unfold.

'You and Peter are famous now for finding her. It's a miracle—our prayers have been answered,' Elly croaked, trying to hold it together.

While they chatted, Briar's cell phone buzzed. She clicked on the text message which was from Al. He needed to talk to her urgently.

'Sorry, Elly. Al, the detective wants to talk to me. I hope it's not bad news about Sandy. I'll get back to you. Would you mind phoning the hospital to find out where we can visit her? Peter is there, but he hasn't phoned yet.'

After Briar finished her call to Elly, she phoned Al who said he needed to come around to discuss a few things that could have an impact on her safety. They agreed to meet first thing in the morning on her half-day off.

🐾 🐾 🐾

'Come on in,' she said to the tall, sun-tanned man in his expensive-looking sunhat and khaki trousers, while she looked at his ring finger and noticed no wedding ring.

'Sorry to arrive so early—I've got a pile of reports waiting for me on my desk. It's only a temporary office where I'm working from at the local station here.'

Briar offered him iced tea which she knew he was partial to. 'I've made toast—have you eaten?'

'Thanks, but I had an early breakfast. The friend I'm staying with near here is a trained chef so I'm well-looked after. Anyway—let's cut to the chase.'

'Oh, sounds ominous,' said Briar, munching on her toast and marmalade.'

'We have reason to believe that Sandy was witness to the killing of the man, Manuel Santos whose body was washed up on Keyhole Rock.'

Briar sat aghast, rubbing her goose-pimpled forearms as Al told about the anonymous cartel member who had seen Sandy's SOS signal.

'He warned that his boss may come looking for her. He had seen the news about Sandy's disappearance and was afraid that if it was her sending the signal, she may die.'

Briar shook her head sideways in disbelief. 'It sounds as though he may know her, otherwise, why would he be so concerned?'

Al sat silent momentarily as though he contemplated whether he should open up too much to Briar.

'I tend to agree with you which means we have another mystery to solve. What connection does the informer have with Sandy?'

Briar slouched forward, leaning on her thighs, shell-shocked by what she was hearing.

'I can't believe this,' she stammered. 'It sounds like something out of a *Rambo* movie. You're saying that he might come to the house to kill her?'

'We don't know what he might do. But the caller told us that he was supposed to deal with her and said he won't do it. It sounds like he had a falling out with the drug boss.'

'Did he name his drug boss?'

'He gave us his name and said he uses several aliases,' said Al.

'Who is it? You can tell me, surely.'

'No, I can't and it's not safe for you to get involved.'

'What am I supposed to do now, then?' Briar blubbered.

'I think it's best to move out of your house for a while until we have apprehended the drug lord running this operation or know that he is out of the country. The Australian and New

Zealand Police have been working on tracking down this cartel for years.'

'You're joking, aren't you? That could take years if he flees the country.' Briar's usual laid-back disposition changed to a state of anxiety as she tried to calm her breathing. She took out a handkerchief to wipe the beads of perspiration that began to show on her temples.

'So I thought after the long-awaited discovery of Sandy and finding her alive, we could finally relax—and now this. What about Sandy—can't she come back home?'

'No—after her discharge we'll have to chaperone her to the house to pack some belongings and move her to a safe place. Have you got a friend you could stay with, away from here?'

Briar leaned on her clasped hands mulling it over.

'Only my parents who live in Green Bay. That would do, I suppose. Sandy could stay with her parents in Parnell for a while. They have plenty of room for her in that huge, flash house of theirs, and she could still paint and write there.'

'Well, we'd better wait until she has recovered before we let her know what the plan is. I'll have to get to the hospital to question her once they allow me to visit.'

Al stood up heading for the door. 'I've got to get back to my office and write my report about the rescue. Thanks for the tea—I'll be in touch soon.'

As he walked to the front steps with Briar in tow, she lurched forward to stop him. 'Wait! There is something else I meant to ask you that I'm in a quandary about.'

He turned and gave her a broad smile. 'Okay—fire away. I must admit it's hard for me to get my head around it all.'

'All this time you never told us if you were able to search out that fellow from the rehab who had been stalking Sandy. You had said you were following the lines of enquiry and not said anything since.'

'I couldn't say anything as we had no real evidence he was stalking her, remember? But yes—we did identify him and wanted to bring him in for questioning, but have been unable to find him.'

Briars face changed colour rapidly, from pink to tomato red. 'What? You still don't know whether he is involved in this crime that Sandy witnessed?'

Al lowered his eyes and hesitated. 'We can't just rush in like a bull at a gate and accuse people without just cause. We have to find him first before we suspect that he is involved in foul play.'

'I thought you were going to see if he was caught on the CCTV,' she said, plonking herself down onto the top step of the porch.

Al sat down next to her. 'We didn't see him on the camera at the surf club which is closest to your home. We did identify a vehicle in the carpark on camera which was registered to a Kingi Walker, a fellow who had been a client at *Living Free*. But this is only circumstantial evidence. Until we talk to Sandy and Kingi himself, we can't progress this line of enquiry until we find him.'

'Unbelievable! It all seems so futile. He can't just have disappeared into thin air,' she retorted.

'I'm sorry, Briar—it has been a lot of stress for you as her flatmate, but it won't be long now. Just concentrate on staying safe. What will you do with the dog while you stay with your parents?'

'I'll ask Peter to take care of him. He's the one who found Sandy together with Sleuth. They're a team and belong together.'

Al gave her more than a warm smile, squeezed her arm and hurried down the steps. As he walked in the direction of the main beach carpark, he called out, 'And thanks again for the iced tea!'

🐕 🐕 🐕

It had been a long morning and Briar was stunned, still trying to get her head around it all. She decided not to go into work and rang up and reported sick, aptly justifying she had a good reason to take a mental health day. She told her manager that Sandy had been rescued and now they were both in danger, although she couldn't yet disclose why. She let them know she would be staying with her relatives, but they were to tell no one and that she was under police protection.

The events of the day robbed her of any motivation to do anything, except taking Sleuth for a walk where she was able to mull things over in her mind to see what clues she could come up with about the identity of the informer.

Unwanted thoughts kept churning over and over in her mind about Kingi Walker. Why was he hanging around that day? Maybe he was involved with the fellow who was washed up at Keyhole Rock and could have been the informer. She knew well the threat of gangs targeting family members if they double-cross them or dob them in. It didn't bear thinking about what they could do to Sandy if they knew she was a witness to a murder or other crime. She stopped in her tracks and slumped down onto a mound of tussock grass staring back in the direction of the lookout and back out at sea while Sleuth nuzzled into her. How could it be that their once peaceful and simple lives had become a whirlpool of angst and chaos overnight? What did this mean? she wondered.

She threw a ball to Sleuth a few times to distract herself from the tension. He dropped it and chased seagulls up and down the shallows until his thick black coat was soaking wet and shook it all over her legs.

'That's alright, Sleuth, dear boy. If only you knew just how precious you are. If you were human, you'd get a medal. I can see why Sandy loves you,' she said, as she clipped him back on his lead and took him home so that she could pack, ready to move away to her parents' house.

Chapter Eighteen

Three Weeks Later

Sandy lay on the couch, propped up with pillows behind her back while Sleuth slobbered over her. The dog hadn't left her side since she had returned home. She had refused to move away out of the area, much to the gross disapproval of the police investigation team, especially Al Crawford and Briar had changed her mind about moving to her parents after all.

'Gee, thanks. What's this?' asked Sandy, as Briar carried in a tray with an omelette and handed it to her.

'Protein with all the goodies to build you back up again after nearly starving,' she said, smiling sweetly.

'Haha. You must be getting sick of cooking for me. I'm such a fussy cow,' said Sandy, smothering her meal with salt and gulping down the freshly squeezed orange juice.

'I think you should go easy on the salt. Your kidneys will have been stressed by dehydration and need to recover,' said Briar, shaking her head.

'Yes, nursie—I get the message.'

'How's the pain today? Need any Panadol?'

'Still niggly when I try to stand. Once I'm on my feet, it's not too bad. Amazing how a cracked pelvis can be so debilitating. At least it wasn't a complete break—only a hairline fracture and, to be honest, the ribs have been more painful.'

Briar placed the bottles of milk she took out of her bag into the fridge door.

'I ran into Al as I came in the gate. He was on his way to the shop and asked how you were—whether you'd changed your mind about moving out of the house. He said you won't have police protection indefinitely if you don't enter a witness protection program.'

'Oh, no—I will say he's persistent. Hope you told him we're coping okay. Anyway, he knows we've got a wonderful neighbourhood watch and everyone's looking out for us. It was good of your father to come over and put up CCTV on our roof and install panic buttons. We'll be okay,' said Sandy standing up and looking out the window. 'No one's hardly going to hassle us with that hulk of a sergeant, PC Plod who keeps stalking us outside the house. I think he's got his eye on you,' she said, winking at her friend.

'Ah—you mean Police Constable Rivers. I know what you mean—he is a bit of a plod, but at least they're trying to look after us.' Their banter was interrupted by Sandy's phone ringing.

'Get that, will you? I don't feel like chatting over the phone right now,' pleaded Sandy.

Briar rushed to answer the phone. 'It's Al—he says it's important that he speaks to you.'

'Oh, alright—I guess I'd better.'

She handed Sandy the phone who turned on the speaker so Briar could hear. After the call they swapped notes.

'Well then—the plot thickens,' said Sandy. 'For a moment I thought he was going to say they'd tracked down Kingi Walker, but he has disappeared without a trace. Anyway, they've got a huge lead in identifying the owner of that yacht, Toledo while it was moored just outside Sydney. They suspect he is the drug baron with all the aliases who operates the cartel, he said, and Manuel Santos has had connections with him the past.'

'That's scary—to think that a dangerous cartel like that has been operating on our doorstep. They're like the mafia. I hope they find him soon.'

Sandy hobbled a few paces across the lounge and then slumped back onto the couch. 'Until they do, I'm going to be super vigilant. But I'm guessing he would have cleared out far away from here now—knowing the cops have found his yacht and confiscated it. He's probably back in South America.'

'Maybe we should have taken up Peter's offer of swapping houses for a while. At least that could throw them off the scent if they want to remove you from the equation,' said Briar, shrugging her shoulders and shaking her head in angst.

'Oh, don't put the wind up me. We just have to be careful when we go out anywhere. Maybe stay around the beach until the police say it's safe,' said Sandy.

Briar sat at the end of the couch next to Sandy, her forehead wrinkling. 'Look—you can't keep confidentiality about this Kingi fellow now—not with our lives at stake. What can you tell me about him? Al had said that the informer stated that you helped him once. Perhaps it was he who blabbed to the police.' Briar finished eating her toast, licking the butter off her fingers.

'Okay—I'll tell you this about Kingi, but you mustn't repeat it to anyone. Only you know this—you and the detective, Al.'

Sandy took a few mouthfuls of the water Briar had placed on the coffee table. 'I went the extra mile to help him as his caseworker, as he had been turning his life around and I kind of felt sorry for him. He'd had a rough childhood having seen his father knocking his mother around.'

Briar grimaced. 'Poor guy. Kids like that suffer from post-traumatic stress.'

'I suppose I only wanted to see the good in him and tried to bring about a reconciliation between him and his partner after she gave birth to his baby during the three months he was in rehab. He appreciated that, and I was a mediator for them.'

Sandy's cheerful countenance changed from one of sadness as her face took on a serious expression.

'I prayed with him once, that God would help him to start a new life—but if he has gone back to crime and using, he'll never see his partner or the baby again. I expect when he came to the beach that day, he was going to ask my help for some reason, and then changed his mind. She has probably left him again. I'd hate to think that he is involved with this cartel as he'll go back to prison and lose his child for good.'

'Wow—this is like one of those detective movies we watch. It's hard to believe it's happening in New Zealand,' said Briar, rubbing the back of her neck and wrinkling her nose.

Sandy sat up again and leaned forward stretching her arms out wide. 'Ooh, my backside. I can't sit down any longer.'

There was a knock at the door.

'That'll be Peter coming to take Sleuth for a walk—I'll get it,' said Sandy, hobbling to the door with a sparkle in her eye.

'Hiya—how are you feeling today?' he asked, before Sleuth almost pushed him to the ground, slobbering over his face.

'Get down, Sleuth!' Sandy touched Peters hand affectionately. 'He just loves you to bits since you helped save me. You are my heroes,' she said blushing.

'Coming in first for a coffee—have you eaten?'

'No, but thanks—I had breakfast around seven. Just couldn't stop all the stuff Al told me last night mulling over in my mind. I usually sleep in on Saturdays, but not today. Did he tell you they found a drug smuggler's yacht from a

South American cartel called the Poderosa? It appears that murder victim Santos has connections with them.'

'I know—I know. Look—let's try to bring some joy into our day and not talk about that stuff for a while. It's starting to get me down, as it's all-consuming, if not depressing.'

'Sorry, Sandy—I understand it must be pretty difficult for you right now,' he said rubbing her arm. Although he'd already given her a long hug when she became conscious in the hospital, he felt it wasn't going to be appropriate right now, although he wanted to squeeze her tight and take care of her.

She beamed a warm smile. 'You've got nothing to be sorry about—not at all. I just don't want to let it take over our lives. The police will get that fellow—don't worry—he won't come here and risk being caught, nor will he send his followers as it is too big an operation to let any of them muck it up.'

She leaned over, and to his surprise, kissed him on the cheek—a long-awaited sign of affection he'd hoped for.

'Let's plan a picnic by the lagoon after home church tomorrow—what do you think? I'll pack some lunch, it's the least I can do.'

Peter touched his cheek, still moist from her kiss. He wanted to return the endearment but felt some restraint was called for, as she was still fragile and he could be over-exuberant at times. 'That sounds great. I'll see you at home church first, anyway.'

'Have fun you two—see you back here soon,' she said, as he attached Sleuth's lead.

Peter along the beach to the designated dog area where he could release Sleuth. This time the dog didn't head for the lookout—that situation was over. The animal did what he was accustomed to do when near the sea, chasing seagulls and frolicking in the waves with Peter at his side.

🐕 🐕 🐕

'I can't wait to start taking Sleuth for a walk myself—I wonder where Peter is,' Sandy said to Briar, pulling the curtain aside and staring along the beach. 'He has gone for a run with him, but should be back by now.'

'Poor Sleuth—he was so distraught when you were missing, but good old Peter diligently took him for a walk or run most days. They are good mates now, those two.'

'Here he comes. We won't take Sleuth on the picnic tomorrow—he'll be too boisterous. I just want a short walk and then sit by the lagoon.'

147

Sandy opened the door as her handsome caller thrust a sizable bunch of colourful flowers in her face before Sleuth whizzed past her, still excited.

'Oh, Peter they're gorgeous. It should be me bearing your gifts.'

'No, honestly—it's my pleasure. I'm so happy to have you back home safely. I saw them at the store when we went passed and couldn't resist.'

'I'll put them in water,' she said, taking a large vase out of the lounge sideboard.

'Mind if I get on? I've got a pile of paperwork to catch up on if I'm going out tomorrow.'

'No, not at all. Thanks for helping out with Sleuth—I greatly appreciate it. See you at home church.'

Chapter Nineteen

Sandy's home church was jubilant she was safely back in the fold. She provided an ample morning tea with food she had purchased from the local café. The welcome home service was held at Barnett Hall. Sandy thanked the small gathering for placing her on their prayer chain. Briar and Elly, who'd offered to help with the morning tea after the service, stayed back to help clean up while Peter whisked Sandy away to prepare for their afternoon together.

'See you at my gate at midday. If you bring those bottles of ginger beer you said you chilled, I have some leftover sandwiches and cake from this morning.'

'Great—see you soon.'

🐈 🐈 🐈

When Peter arrived, he appeared excited to spend time alone with Sandy. Before long the two friends strolled around the lagoon, full of the joys of life as if their recent, life-shattering upheaval never happened. Sandy couldn't walk far, but while she ambled along in the delightful company of her rescuer, she experienced no pain, just oblivion and she felt safe.

'We're in luck—the park bench over there is free for once. I'll go grab it,' Peter said, as he carried their chilly bin to the seat while Sandy hobbled along several paces behind.

'Come—plonk yourself down here,' he said, patting the seat. 'I'll play the mother.' He opened the chilly bin and unpacked the sandwiches, each beautifully wrapped in pink serviettes from the morning tea. 'Mmm—pink,' he muttered, winking at Sandy.

'Well that's all I could find to wrap them in,' she said, as she reached over to take the soft drink bottle he handed her.

'I tell you—when you've been on the brink of starvation and near death, anything like this is pure bliss, no matter what package it presents itself,' said Sandy, while Peter's penetrating gaze searched her changing facial expression.

They said little to each other while they ate and drank, quietly enjoying the peaceful surroundings apart from the occasional sound of the water birds on the lagoon.

Once she had eaten, Sandy pulled off her shoes and tip-toed over to the water's edge, dipping her toes in the cool water. Peter caught her up, and when she took a few steps too many, she slipped, almost toppling into the murky water, save for Peter. He lurched forward enveloping her around the waist with his brawny, tanned arms that saved her for the second time.

'Whew, that was close,' he said, reluctantly releasing her. 'That wouldn't have been too pleasant falling face down in all that duck poo,' he said, chuckling.

'Thanks, Peter,' she said, shuffling back to the park bench to grab her beach sandals. 'I'm still a bit unstable on my legs until I build up muscle strength again.'

'Well, you just keep up those physio exercises and get fit. I want us to start hiking again—and no more taking off on your own on those rugged clifftop paths, eh?'

They packed up and slowly walked back to Sandy's house, but this time, Sandy reached out for Peter's hand, and for the first time, he wrapped his hand around hers and kept it there until her house was in view and then she pulled it away.

'I don't suppose I want everyone to see us like this or they'll think we're an item,' she said, averting his gaze.

'Wait,' he said, clutching her wrist, 'Aren't we?'

Before they arrived back on the path that led to her home, he planted a lingering kiss on her lips and then walked on smiling, beaming from ear to ear with Sandy at his side with the look of a stunned mullet.

After he walked her to her gate, he handed her the chilly bin.

'Coming in for a while? Briar's going to her parents tonight as she has the day off tomorrow. Stay for dinner, if you like.'

'Are you sure? You must be tired, seeing it's the first time you've been out walking since your discharge from hospital.'

Sandy took his hand and led him inside. 'We've still got a Beef Lasagne in the fridge leftover from last night and some of Briar's yummy apple crumble.'

'Okay—you insist, but I can't stay late if you don't mind. I've got a client arriving in the morning early, and I need to print off a few things before he arrives.'

They had previously shared their views on celibacy before marriage, but he had to make a concentrated effort at not placing himself in temptation's way, and so did she, he guessed. But for now, a tasty home-cooked meal and snug chit-chat on the couch for afters would have to suffice.

Chapter Twenty

Sandy had sent Peter home after he'd started nodding off on her lap, and she was tired after such an eventful day.

Sleuth had already taken himself off to sleep on his mat in her bedroom where he watched over her each night. A strong, south-westerly wind was developing that caused the 1960s heritage home to shake, but she'd got used to it over the years. She'd forgotten to close the drapes and felt exposed with the light on and standing in full view. As she got up to close them, she heard a rustle coming from somewhere in the house. It was a different sound from the norm—perhaps it was that jolly opossum on the roof again. That's why she'd shut the door of her bedroom while Sleuth was in there sound asleep. If he woke to hear that creature on the roof again, he would go berserk and she just couldn't cope with that right now.

She heard the sound again and felt the need to check. For a moment she sat back on the couch in the lounge keeping her eye on the panic button concealed from view under the kitchen island in the open-plan kitchen. She felt secure in the fact that she and Briar both had one installed in their bedrooms. Perhaps she was just super vigilant and nervous since witnessing the midnight drama at Whites Beach.

This time it sounded different, like background noise from the movie she'd starting watching on TV, but when she muted the sound, there was a definite tapping this time. It appeared to emanate from the dining room, which made her skin crawl. As she stood up and leaned an ear towards the sound, she recollected pushing the window open when she was cooking and had forgotten to close it. Although all the windows in the house had been replaced with aluminium joinery and security screens, it unnerved her. Edging herself slowly through the lounge door, she peered around the doorpost. She felt the artery in her neck pulsating when suddenly the dark silhouette of someone at the window outside in a howling gale called, 'Sandy, it's me—Kingi—Kingi Walker,' as he tapped on the glass pane.

She stood motionless, her throat tightened with angst as she didn't recognise the face, although she knew the voice. 'Please, Sandy—I mean you no harm—I just want you to listen,' he said, pushing his face into the crack between the open window and the security screen.

Should she run to the bedroom and let Sleuth deal with him? He would go crazy and try to protect her.

'I don't recognise you as Kingi Walker,' she said, about to head for the panic button.

'I've cut off my dreads,' he said, shining a small torch on his face.

Sandy squinted, craning her neck to get a clearer view from where she stood.

'Well, I'm not letting you in—you'll have to talk out there. Why are you here—the police are looking for you?'

He pressed his head in closer, and in the light reflecting from the lounge, she could see the telltale chain tattoo about his neck and a small, thick scar above his right eyebrow. When she peered closer, the sight of a handsome tanned face, black hair with short back and sides, and a thick moustache startled her.

'I know they are—and I'm in deep trouble for snitching on the drug cartel, Poderosa which I was once involved with and now leaving to start a new life. When I heard you had been rescued from the cliffs at Whites Beach, I knew it was you who sent an SOS signal. You must have been a witness to the murder of Manuel Santos, weren't you?'

'You've come here to kill me, haven't you? I'm calling the police.'

'Wait!' he shouted. 'Stop, please. I want to do you, of all people, no harm. I informed the police anonymously that I was afraid you'd die if I didn't tell them where you were after all you did to help me and my family.'

'Thank you ... what's going to happen to you now? Surely the drug baron and his associates will have your head on a platter now that you've dobbed him in.'

'They've got no proof I said anything. It could be a random witness who informed the police. I told them the exact island in the Pacific where Carlos Rodriguez will be stopping to load the next shipment on another of his vessels that has arrived from Colombia to transfer to a boat in Australian waters. He is a drug smuggler and hitman, but not the leader of the cartel. I can identify the real one, but not until I have a guarantee of police leniency as a trade for my information. Often the cops will do that to get what they what, in other words—they let a small fish go to catch a big one. They are going to search his boat with his next haul, and make it appear as a routine check by coast guards in international waters. They have already confiscated the yacht, Toledo in the Bay Of Islands, but haven't caught Carlos yet.'

'They'll probably come after you if he gets caught,' said Sandy.

'My partner and baby are living down south, and I'd like to show her that I'm going to turn my life around, but I have to change my identity for a while. We may have to live overseas until we're safe. If I get caught, I've decided to give the police a confidential, unsigned written statement—evidence that will destroy the drug empire of the Poderosa and put him behind bars for the rest of his life, only if they'll do a trade-off and offer me and my family protection. That's only if they arrest me which they can't do without evidence that I'm involved.'

'I don't understand—why did you go back to a life of crime after rehab? I heard you discharged yourself when you were doing so well.'

'I intended to make a new start, especially for my mother who is staying with family down the line, and my partner and our baby. But on my release from rehab my old drug boss Carlos who I once worked with in Australia, said I owed him, and if I didn't dive for this massive drug haul on his yacht, the Toledo, he would hurt my family. I didn't owe him anything—he is deluded.'

'But you still haven't said why you are here?'

'I need to know what you told the police you could see from the cliff to corroborate my story and to tell you that Carlos is going to be arrested any day soon, as he is on the crew on this next shipment heading to Sydney through the Pacific. I made sure the police would know exactly his location. He'll be going away for life for drug trafficking and for killing my friend, Manuel Santos in cold blood. But you still need to watch your back. He has friends in high places, which I can't discuss with you yet.'

Sandy was dumbfounded trying to get her head around this barrage of information thrust at her. She was in two minds. One said she could trust him, as while he was in rehab she saw his soft, caring side—and the other says drug addicts and ex-cons are like dogs who return to their own vomit. Now she had to follow her instinct that she should give him a chance at redeeming himself.

'It was hard for me to see anything clearly as I was too far away and groggy from the pain I was in. I saw a man at the helm and a tall, hefty bloke who committed the assault. Afterwards, the two men dragged the body out of the water and slung him back into the boat. I witnessed the whole event but I couldn't see the faces, or give a description as the scene was almost a blur, sorry. Were you one of them?'

'I was driving the boat and told Carlos not to hurt anyone as it wasn't part of the plan. I dived and transported the cocaine from the rudder compartment onto the runner boat.'

Sandy shook her head in disgust.

'So you couldn't identify me from where you were up on the cliff?'

'No, I couldn't identify anyone—I was too far away.'

'Whew, that's a relief. That's all I wanted to know. So the police have no proof I was involved.'

'I have asked the rehab for copies of the counselling reports you wrote so I can give them to the police if I am arrested.'

Sandy started to feel uncomfortable about Kingi hanging around so long. There was nothing she could do for him.

'Sorry, Kingi, but you'll have to leave now. My dog will be waking up and if he hears you, he'll go berserk and annoy the neighbours.'

'Sure—a friend dropped me off nearby. I'll message him on my phone and he can pick me up down the road.'

'Good thing you dropped the hood of your jacket in time and I recognised your voice as I almost hit the alarm that would signal the local police constable who is on call here at night.'

'Thanks, heaps, Sandy. I won't let you down. I'm heading south tomorrow evening. My partner and my mother have taken our baby to stay with family down there until I get things sorted out. I purchased some land on the West coast of the South Island and plan to grow tea tree, as there's a lucrative market there for Manuka honey. I'm going to marry my partner—make an honest woman out of her. She's giving me the last chance to redeem myself and we'll change our names. I'll get a message to you someday to let you know about my new life.' he said, slipping his hood back on his head. 'I'll push the window closed if you want to lock it after I've gone.'

As he pushed the window shut, the noise disturbed Sleuth who began growling and whining from the bedroom.

Without delay, Kingi darted off. Sandy locked the window and let Sleuth out of the room. He rushed into the dining room, sniffing and looking around like a true retriever and then whined in disappointment that his search returned void.

Sandy sat back on the couch with mixed feelings about Kingi. She didn't know whether she should be ecstatic that he turned up with this confession or disturbed that he had come to her house. Should she go to the police? As she sat back, mentally exhausted from the day's events, Sleuth lay his head on her feet, as if he understood and offered her comfort.

It was not such a great end to an enrapturing day as Kingi's visit had put a damper on the happy bubble that had encapsulated her after Peter had left. She wasn't sure whether to tell him about it, but he would only press her to report it straight away. She did feel a great sense of relief that, for the first time since her discharge from hospital, she understood what had transpired that dreadful night when she witnessed the ugly slaying of Manuel Santos.

Lying in bed, she prayed for a good outcome for Kingi and his family—that he would not only avoid arrest but also be safe from his enemies. She was convinced he had changed.

As she lay there digesting the barrage of information her visitor had bombarded her with, her thoughts darted to Peter, as he seemed to be her significant other right now apart from her parents and she couldn't worry them with this, especially her mother who just wouldn't be able to cope. Peter would always help her make the right decision about what to do. But was she ready to go to the police, as that's what he would suggest? He was someone she could trust, and she respected his opinions, but this time, she wanted to wait and give Kingi a chance to get far away. He deserved that break.

That night Sleuth uncharacteristically took the liberty to lie across the end of her bed instead of sleeping on his mat. Perhaps he sensed that she was in more danger than she realised.

Chapter Twenty-one

Peter heard a vehicle pull up in his driveway. He wasn't expecting anyone and poked his head out the window to see who it was. A dated jeep covered in mud appeared and an elderly man opened the door and stood looking around.

'Ah—that's the old recluse, Jock,' he muttered to himself. 'I thought he would never come.'

He turned off his computer and wandered out the front of the house before Jock knocked on the door.

'My goodness—what brings you here? Good to see you, Jock,' Peter said, shaking his hand. 'Coming in for a coffee?'

'I'll come in but I don't touch that coffee stuff. Bad for the stomach. Tea will suit me just fine.'

While Peter made the tea, he saw out of the corner of his eye from the kitchen that Jock was intrigued by the paintings in his lounge.

'Lion Rock, eh? A pretty good painting that one.'

'That was painted by the girl I told you about who had gone missing. But you do know she has been found alive and well, don't you?' He handed Jock a biscuit. 'You're in luck—Sandy baked me a batch of Anzac biscuits,' he said, handing the plate to Jock.

Jock smiled and took one, dunking it in his tea.

'I'm not a complete hermit, mate. I do have a radio and listen to the news.'

'Then you will have heard that the fella who was washed up on Keyhole Rock was part of a Brazilian drug cartel called the Poderosa.'

'Yep—heard that too. In fact—that's why I'm here. You asked me lots of questions that day you and that young woman came to see me. I just wasn't ready to talk about it.'

Peter's stomach somersaulted. Was he hearing right—did Jock know a lot more than he had been letting on?

Peter swallowed the rest of his tea and tried to gain composure so as not to pressure Jock and frighten him off.

'I don't understand, Jock. Are you wanting to tell me you know something about what happened to that fellow?'

His visitor squirmed in his seat and sniffed loudly.

'The cops have been asking for people to come forward who have any information about this Santos fellow and his demise. They are offering a huge reward, but it's not that I'm interested in. I don't want the drug trafficking scum in my neighbourhood or anywhere near here and will do what I can to prevent it so I can live in peace.'

Peter felt a band of tension form around the top of his head. Is this man another witness to the murder? He waited then poured himself and Jock another mug of tea and sat drinking it quietly waiting.

Jock shuffled around and then began. 'I didn't tell you the whole truth about what I saw. You remember I said I often go down to Whites Beach to swim, or in my case to wash. Well, that night, it was so hot I couldn't sleep and went off down there to take a dip and cool off. It was such a bright, moonlit night—you know, one of those clear nights where the sky appears full of diamonds. I was almost at the end of the track that comes out by the dunes when I heard a soft motor as a small boat appeared. I gathered it was just a couple of fishermen. Apart from the mast light at the bow of the boat, I could see a dim light in the cabin and two men standing arguing on the deck while another chap with long dreadlocks stood at the helm. Although a couple of fishing rods protruded from either side of the boat, it all looked a bit suspicious, so I hung back behind a tree and watched. The boat stayed in the shallows while the men continued their dispute and then suddenly the tall man with the thick, bald head struck the shorter fellow hard in the back of his head with his fist. He went flying over the side of the boat, knocking his head hard as he fell. I even heard the thud when he struck the side of the boat.'

Peter began jotting down some notes.

'Hey—don't go writing this down. I don't want to end up having to testify in court—I want none of that drama in my life.'

Peter obliged by putting his writing pad and pen aside. 'Please carry on, Jock. It's very interesting—it'll make for a great novel.'

'When the chap fell in the water, I didn't see him get up and within a few minutes, the man with dreads and the tall thug stepped into the water and dragged him out—slinging him into the boat. Then they revved the motor and took off out into the dark yonder.'

Peter sat shaking his head. 'Unbelievable! You witnessed the whole murder then?'

Jock's eyes widened as he became agitated. 'I didn't realise it was a murder at that point. I didn't know the guy they slung into the boat was dead or unconscious, or that they dumped him in the sea afterwards.'

'Why didn't you report it to the police? The only witness they have is Sandy and she couldn't see much from where she lay—just mere silhouettes.'

'I live alone and guessed they might come looking for me if I spill the beans, and I couldn't prove that they actually killed him.'

'Well, whatever happened afterwards, you were still a witness to the assault on Santos. Do you think you could give the police a witness statement? It would speed up the process of them catching that psycho, Carlos Rodriguez. Would you be able to describe him at all?'

'I suppose ... but I don't want them to come after me and cut me up into small pieces. Next thing they'll find my bits and bobs washed up on the beach in a suitcase. You know how dangerous that lot are.'

Peter shuddered as he considered Sandy's safety. He was desperate to find another witness, and this was his breakthrough. His eyes remained fixated on Jock's face as he tried not to imagine what he had just said. He had to convince him to go forward as a witness—that would take the heat off poor Sandy and if the thugs know that somebody else was able to describe their appearance, perhaps they would leave Sandy alone.

Jock sat pulling at his fingers nervously. 'I need to know they won't disclose my name or address, otherwise, I won't do it.'

'You don't have to give your identity. They will call you an anonymous witness, such as Witness A. They could put you into the Witness Protection Program.'

'Oh, is that right? Maybe I could oblige if that's the case. Will you write the statement? You have to give me your word you won't identify me—promise?'

'Of course, I give you my word. How about tomorrow? I'll take the statement to DI Crawford and he can move forward on it. If it gets to court, they may ask you to do a video interview and dub your voice.'

'I hope it's going to be worth it and they can catch the criminals. We don't want this trash in our community so the sooner they arrest them the better.'

Peter walked over and patted him on the shoulder. 'You've no idea what a breakthrough it is to have you come forward. Thanks for trusting me and coming to see me, Jock.'

'No worries mate. I could see the anguish in your face that day you came asking if I knew anything. You were so upset about this young woman Sandy going missing that I guessed she is somebody really special in your life.'

Peter's neck flushed. 'You can say that again. I would have been devastated if anything had happened to her,' he said with a half-smile.

'So you're hoping I'll be the key witness and keep the heat off her?'

Peter shoved his hands in his pockets and looked down at his feet. He had been caught out.

'Sandy was too high up the cliff to see their faces, but she is the only witness that have. They need someone to come forward who could help identify the men and you are the one.'

Deep down, Peter knew that wasn't the real reason why he was looking for another witness. He had an ongoing concern for her safety.

'So what do you want me to do?' asked Jock as he headed for the door.

'I'll type out a statement on the computer from the notes I wrote, just as you told it to me and I'll drop by your place tomorrow morning to get you to check it. Can you read through the notes I've written before you go, just to make sure I've got it right?' Peter handed him the note pad.

Jock perused the document and handed it back to him. 'Well, you'd better make sure they don't ever find out who I am. There's no way I want to up sticks and move away to some God-forsaken place so the gangsters won't find me. I'm too old for an upheaval like that.'

'Trust me—you have my word. I'll see to that. They might want you to do a remote witness interview if the judge doesn't accept an anonymous witness statement in writing. But it is all done with anonymity and they dub your voice,' said Peter before he waved him off in the driveway.

Chapter Twenty-two

A Month Later

Peter took Sandy's hand and led her across the dunes towards Lion Rock, ready to do the climb for the first time since her accident. Elly had gone on ahead as Sandy had to tread carefully and at a snail's pace until her legs became stronger, although she was completely healed.

When they gathered together at the summit, they were welcomed by an autumn, dawn sunrise with a sweeping backdrop of orange sky as the three friends sat looking out at sea.

After the three of them got lost in a period of contemplative meditation, Sandy spoke up.

'DS Crosby dropped by yesterday with some great news that should be on the television tonight. That drug smuggler, Carlos has been apprehended in the Pacific by Australian Border Security. They found large residues of cocaine on board his yacht, but whatever the shipment was he carried on board had already been removed. They have no proof he was smuggling but have confiscated his boat. If they find he is guilty of Santos's murder, he will be tried in New Zealand where the crime took place. But if it's only possession of Class A drugs, he will be tried in Sydney as they were in Australian waters.'

'Oh—you mean that cartel leader, Rodriguez,' said Elly. 'I read that he is also a hitman and has committed several revenge murders. The police have had him under surveillance for years, waiting for enough evidence to nail him. Scary stuff though.'

'I know—that's why Ben Crosby wanted to reassure me that if he is convicted, he'll get multiple life sentences and never get out of prison. I can finally sleep peacefully knowing he's not getting back into this country,' said Sandy.

'So what about your witness statement? I hope you won't have to go over there and stand up in court?' asked Peter, gaping with eyes on stalks.

'No—I have written a confidential witness statement that will be produced in court that won't have my name or contact details on it. I won't need to be there and I'm testifying about the assault, not the drug trafficking,' she said, as

Peter squeezed her hand with relief. 'But they also had an anonymous witness statement from someone else—another local person who was going for a swim the night of the assault and saw the whole thing unfold. He could even describe the assailants.'

Sandy couldn't hide her lack of ease. Furrows formed in her brow as she sat biting her bottom lip while Peter was bursting to say he knew who the witness was, but he had been sworn to secrecy.

'What's wrong—is there something else you want to tell us—you look worried,' said Peter, putting his arm around her.

'Al said one of the men had dreads and from the witness's description, it could have been Kingi Walker, and he was trying to extract more information from me. He seemed unusually persuasive, almost desperate to find him.'

Sandy hadn't gone to the police about the visit she had from Kingi. She hoped he would have been able to disappear and start a new life as she'd decided he was telling the truth about having been forced to dive. She too was sworn to secrecy.

'I just don't know what's happening with that fellow, Kingi—I haven't heard from him again. I hope he and his family are okay.'

After they wound up their fellowship time and made their way to the bottom of Lion Rock, Elly squirmed—seeing she was now playing gooseberry with this new couple. The status quo of their little group had now changed with this new romance blossoming to the extent that she no longer felt comfortable meeting up on the rock anymore. It had been great, all single and on the same wavelength, but now things were different. It was time she had a boyfriend of her own but tucked away, living and working in this tiny beach settlement, it was never going to happen.

'Sorry, guys—hate to break up the party, but I've got to start work early this morning. It was an awesome sunrise today and thanks for the fellowship. I'm having to do some early shifts a few days a week so won't always be able to meet on Lion Rock.'

Sandy darted a surreptitious glance at Peter and sensing the disquiet that Elly must be feeling took hold of her arm. 'We've had someone else enquiring whether they could join us on Lion Rock some mornings—DS Ben Crosby. He said he loves the Piha sunrises and showed me his flash new Nikon camera,' she said, darting Peter a wry smile.

'Oh, did he now?' said Elly, her face suddenly lighting up. She had developed a soft spot for Ben that had not gone unnoticed by her two friends. 'That's okay with me.'

Sandy and Peter tried not to make eye contact with each other, as Elly's agenda had become far too obvious.

She skipped across the dunes to the surf club, her demeanour taking on a new slant, while Peter took Sandy's hand and held her close walking her home.

'Time to come in for a quick cuppa before you start work?' Sandy asked Peter.

'Sorry, but I've got a new contract I need to start on. It's got to be finished by Friday, but I can see you tonight, though.'

'I was just thinking—imagine if Elly and Ben get together. That just leaves Briar.'

'I thought she was dating Elly's brother, Tim. How's that going? I thought she had quite a crush on him.'

'Slowly—I think. It's early days, and she doesn't say much about him. I don't think he's in any great hurry to settle down, so she won't rush it.'

'Still, she'll do alright with that one now he's a successful barrister,' said Peter.

'It's good he got out of the police force. I would rather be a lawyer's wife than a policeman's anytime.'

'Do architects fall into the lawyer category?' he asked, with smiling eyes.

'I'll catch you up tonight. Would you like to come for a meal? I'll cook for a change,' said Peter.

'Wow—that will be a change alright. Sure, I'll be around at six. I might have some news by then. Al is coming to see me after I finish work this afternoon about my witness statement for the court hearing.'

As she shut the door, she was glad Peter didn't pressurise her to tell what knew about Kingi. It was difficult keeping secrets, but she couldn't bear thinking that if she spilt the beans about his confession, he would go to prison because of her.

Chapter Twenty-three

Al arrived on the dot, just as Sandy had finished for the day in her art studio. She put the kettle on while Al had already taken a seat in the lounge.

'Tea?' she asked, as she set the tray with tea and biscuits on the coffee table.

'Yes, thanks—milk, no sugar.'

There was something different about him—his countenance had changed. Instead of his usual bubbly self, his facial features revealed harsh lines around his mouth and eyes, his mouth downturned, almost in a scowl.

'Everything alright?' she asked, searchingly.

'I hope so. We need to get things underway before this court hearing starts in the next two weeks.'

She picked up on the passive-aggressive tone in his voice.

'What would you like me to do? I've already given you all the information I can,' she asserted, swallowing a lump in her throat.

Al took two chocolate chippie biscuits and put them on the table, next to his mug.

'I need more information about this Kingi Walker who was a client of yours in rehab. We need to track down his family and try to find where he is living right now. The rehab wasn't able to release any of the counselling records without a court order so you need to tell me as much as you know about him.'

Sandy felt pressured, and she didn't like the look in Al's eyes, as if he knew she was hiding something and it angered him for some reason.

'I keep telling you—it's confidential ... the records I mean. I don't know where his family lives.'

Al slurped back the rest of his tea, finished his biscuits and took out his notepad. 'Are you sure you haven't seen him since he left rehab?'

Sandy hesitated. 'No since his last visit ... um ... I mean since he tried to visit my house that day he was in front of my house.'

Sandy hated lying or being deceitful, but this was to save someone's life so she justified it.

Al gave her a momentary silent stare. 'Right—let's get this witness statement—and make it as accurate as possible. If this guy is a murderer, I'm going to get him.'

With this last comment, Sandy felt a load of angst press against her chest wall, causing her to hyperventilate. She stood up quickly. 'I've got to open a window and get some fresh air—it's stuffy inside today.' She stood looking out the open window, trying to get her head around the sudden discomfort she was feeling around Al for the first time, and she wished that Peter was there with her, or even Briar. She poured herself another cup of tea and sat down.

'More tea?'

He thrust the document at her to read. 'No thanks—let's just get on. Anything to add to this?' he said, abruptly.

She sat perusing the notes he'd written, her hand visibly shaking while holding the paper.

'That seems to be everything, except that you haven't said that the three men were a blur— all I could see were silhouettes and therefore unable to describe any of them.'

'So you didn't see that one of them had dreads?'

'No! I did not,' she retorted, her sharpness expressing her defensiveness.

'Okay then. I'll take this back to the station and get it typed up. It appears that Carlos

Rodriguez will go to trial in Sydney in about two weeks for drug trafficking, but we still don't have any evidence to nail him for the murder of Manuel Santos. And getting back to Kingi Walker—I thought your involvement with him in rehab may have shed some light on his personal life.'

Sandy couldn't understand why he was so focused on Kingi when the one he should have been obsessed about was Carlos. But she was determined to throw the heat off him for as long as possible to help him get far away.

Al stood up and for an instant looked her up and down. He didn't smile once during his visit this time. Something had got under his skin.

'Are you still working from Piha Station?' Sandy asked, hoping he wasn't going to be in her face for much longer.

'Yes, temporarily. It was only supposed to be during the time you were missing, but since there has been a murder, I've been busy here and it's far easier to stay near the beach, especially while I'm getting witness statements. We may have to use a remote witness video with you if you're to remain anonymous. Your voice will be dubbed.'

'I don't mind. I just want to get it over and done with.'

Al walked to the door, picking up his ostentatious hat on the way. 'If you think about anything else that might help us track Kingi Walker, don't hesitate to phone me, okay? I think you'd better stay around Piha until all this blows over and we have the culprits locked up.'

For the first time since she had met Al, she had felt ill at ease with his visit. His warmth and charm at gone. Perhaps it was never really there.

'I get that, but I just need to drive into Titirangi Village to New World tomorrow for my weekly groceries, and maybe grab some lunch there. It's a break from hanging around here, as I haven't been out much since my accident and … the murder.'

He glared at her. 'Well—that's up to you, but you had better be careful. You're still vulnerable— Oh—and thanks for the tea and biscuits,' he muttered, heading out the door and back to the carpark.

She remembered Peter was cooking for her which put a smile on her face and she hurried off to freshen up and change her clothes. Tonight was a real date, and she needed a lift.

Sleuth had to be fed and today she had no time to walk him but tomorrow she would make up for it. She placed his meat in a bowl, changed his water and raced out the door.

Chapter Twenty-four

The next morning, DS Ben Crosby arrived much earlier than usual at the station to catch up on a pile of reports Al had thrust at him the day before to type up. When he arrived in the carpark he was surprised to see Al's car was there already.

He walked towards the office stopping in the hallway, as he overheard Al on the phone. 'Yep, I'll be there,' he said to the caller. 'What time are you going down to the beach for a swim? I'll wait for you up the top. Okay, see you then—I'll have the document with me.'

Ben was baffled and hesitated before he walked into the office. Al almost jumped out of his skin when he appeared.

'Oh, hello—you're here early. I ... I'm just catching up on a bit of paperwork as I've got a lot of business to get done today. I've got to call into Headquarters at the West Auckland Station to file my reports on the Santos case and see how far they've got with Carlos's court hearing. Oh—

and I thought you might want to know that, after this week, I'll be working back at Headquarters, a forty-minute drive from Piha, but you may as well continue here, seeing you live at the beach.'

Al sat perusing the few witness statements he had in his hand.

'Okay, no worries—I'm cool with that,' mumbled Ben.

'Do you think we have enough to nail him?' he asked.

'Who are you talking about—Carlos? You've read them—what do you think?' he snapped.

Ben was taken aback by his acidity. 'The phone informer—can you use him as a witness too? I mean ... how do you know he didn't just have a vendetta against Carlos and was lying? Carlos would have plenty of enemies.'

'Yes, I gather that Ben—I'm not stupid,' he retorted with a nasty tone in his voice.

'I hear you're keen to climb Lion Rock with Sandy and her friends at dawn each morning—Peter told me. Be careful—Sandy is a key witness. If you do go, try and pry out of her as much information you can get on Kingi Walker.'

'Why is that? According to the anonymous witness, it was Carlos who smacked Santos over the head. He'll be up for murder on that statement. That witness is prepared to do a remote video interview. We have no evidence Kingi was involved in any of this.'

Al's eyes turned dark. Ben cringed as he began to see another side to his colleague and superior.

'He is involved and I'll track him down and prove it. Here—type these out. I'll need a copy of each. After that, contact the CIB and see how far they're at with Carlos's court hearing. Tell them we have two witnesses who will have to do remote witness videos. I have some business to do out West and will be away for a few hours.'

'Yep, sure can. I'm not the only one who wants that mongrel put away for life, so all the witnesses the better,' said Ben, not knowing that he just caused Al's blood to seethe.

🐈 🐈 🐈

That morning, after a pleasant, romantic and relaxing evening the previous night with Peter following Al's visit, Sandy looked forward to the long drive through the Waitakere Ranges on Scenic Drive to do her weekly grocery shopping in Titirangi Village. Her stomach was still full of the Moroccan Meatballs and couscous Peter had so proudly served her, one of his special gourmet delights. Today was her day off and she had ample time to stop for lunch in one of her favourite cafes.

After letting Sleuth out in the yard after their early morning walk, she filled her drink bottle and grabbed an apple to put in the car in preparation for her trip. She reached into her Toyota Rav4 and took out a cloth to wipe the autumn dew from the window. Sleuth loved coming on outings with her and she always felt guilty when leaving him behind, but this time he would be a nuisance in the village. She would take him next time she visits her parents in Parnell where she could walk him along the boardwalk by the waterfront.

She turned on the engine and the starter motor wouldn't budge. 'Oh no, not again!' Flustered she tried again and again and on the third try it started. It was time to get it looked, as since her setback with being out of work for so long, she hadn't been able to sell paintings or work in the restaurant where she could earn extra money. But now she was back at work, she decided she could afford to get one of the local mechanics to look at it.

'Whew,' she muttered, 'At last.' The car lurched forward, and she took off happily up the long and windy road that led to the Scenic Drive.

She loved this trip—the dense rain forest with native trees, especially her favourite kauri and rimu trees towering above the road and the ponga trees with their lime-green and silver fern fronds. It was a perfect autumn day with a clear blue, cloudless sky and warm sun. She opened her window and breathed in the sweet, woody fragrance of the forest, glad to be alive. What more could she want—a good life living in her beach community and a blossoming romance. She felt blessed.

A single parking spot caught her attention in the carpark opposite the tiny supermarket under the trees. She decided to have coffee at the little café that looked out at the sea in the distance, overlooking more native forest.

Mmm—Black forest gateau—I haven't tasted that in years.

The man behind the counter smiled at her. 'I can tell you it's as delicious as it looks—freshly made today.'

'Yes, please, I can't come all the way here without sampling that. I'd like a flat white in a mug with one shot if that's okay.'

'Sure is—coming right up. I'll bring it to you.'

Sandy took a seat by the window where there was one table left that captured the spectacular view. She could remember visiting the café with her parents as a child when they lived at nearby French Bay, and the cakes were the one thing she could recall. Looks like they've kept the tradition, she thought.

'Here you are, young lady ... wait ... aren't you the lass who went missing from Piha recently ... the one who was found alive?'

Sandy's cheeks went red. She was hoping she could go unnoticed and not have to answer all the questions.

'Yep—that's me, all safe and sound, but I'd rather not talk about it today—it's all they ever talk about at Piha and I've escaped for the day.'

The man looked embarrassed, as he placed the tray in front of her. 'I'm sorry—didn't mean to upset you. I recognised your face from the news on TV.'

'No—don't be sorry—you were just being friendly ... I'm looking forward to the cake ... did you bake it?' she asked, changing the subject.

'No—the place would shut down if they let me loose in the kitchen. It's our gourmet chef, Bob—he's our asset. You enjoy—have a great afternoon,' he said, hurrying off and leaving Sandy in peace.

She found it hard to tear herself away from the ambience of the café and the special view, but she had a load of grocery shopping to get, especially now she regularly cooked for Peter during the week. She was grateful that she didn't have to shop for Briar too, but they were both independents.

The shopping took longer than she'd expected, as she'd forgotten her list. Afterwards, she trundled across the road at the traffic lights, overloaded by bags of heavy groceries. Now she wished she'd parked in the supermarket's small car park, even though a car had banged into the back of her last time she'd done that.

She turned on the key in the ignition and once again the engine coughed and spluttered. To her surprise, it started on the second attempt.

Sandy was sad to leave the village. It held nostalgic memories for her and sometimes she'd thought of moving back there. But she loved the beach and being involved with the surf club where her brother was once well-known as a champion lifesaver until his death saving a child.

While she coasted along the Scenic Drive on her way home, she noticed a grey Holden in her rear vision mirror trailing behind in the distance. It seemed to have stayed behind her the whole way along the road since she had left the village. Suddenly as she veered around a deceptive bend, a mother duck with her babies waddled out onto the road until she was almost on top of them. She slammed on the brakes, forcing the vehicle to a standstill inches from the wildlife. 'Shucks! I nearly killed them. I've got to get them out of the road,' she cried, jumping out of the car and standing like a madwoman beckoning the ducks to follow her into the bush while watching for oncoming traffic. As the ducks disappeared into the thicket towards a nearby stream, Sandy's heart was still racing when she tried to start the car. After three frustrating attempts, there was no life. It just grunted and died each time. Then out of the corner of her eye, she spied the grey car which had pulled up behind her vehicle. She was jumpy, not trusting anyone since her accident and kept her car doors locked, picking up her cell phone ready to call Peter—until she recognised the hat and the voice and rolled down her window.

'Well, well—fancy seeing you here,' said Al with a sly grin. 'Having a bit of trouble are you?' he asked, leaning on the pillar of the open window.

'Sorry I can't help with the car—I'm useless with these modern vehicles and they all have computers which makes it even more difficult. But I can give you a ride back to the beach. Release the handbrake and pull into the shoulder of the road,' he demanded.

After she'd done what he'd said, she was at loggerheads whether to jump into the car with him or phone Peter and ask him to fetch her. But she remembered he had appointments with two important clients and decided not to bother him.

She capitulated and stepped into the passenger side, although she preferred to sit in the back, but didn't want to aggravate him. As she climbed into the passenger seat, her heart missed a beat when her eyes flashed to a blue cell phone and handgun in the open glove box which Al slammed shut.

'You had better get the car towed back to the beach as soon as possible before the toerags around here start dismantling it.'

'Thanks, I appreciate the ride,' said Sandy, still shaking from her discovery.

Before they reached the end of Scenic Drive, Al turned off into a small blind side road and pulled up. Sandy's heart somersaulted into her mouth. She could hardly speak.

'What ... why are you stopping ... anything wrong?'

Al turned to her, his eyes ablaze. 'Well, now that you ask ... there is. It's you interfering with this process of trying to capture Santos's killer and protecting Kingi Walker. It's not going to do you any good. I can arrest you for perverting the course of justice.'

Sandy froze. She felt bullied. Why had this man turned on her? Up until now, she and her friends had put their trust in him, but now it was as if he was no longer on their side.

Her throat felt like she had swallowed needles. She grasped her drink bottle and took large gulps almost choking from the tension in her throat muscles.

'It's not true. You can't recriminate the man on circumstantial evidence—even I know that.'

Al scowled. 'Oh—we are getting defensive and I guess that you're hiding something. You don't want to come to a sticky end washed up on the beach somewhere like Manuel Santos now do you? That's what happens when you don't play the game.'

What does he mean to play the game? Sandy's head was spinning and her heart thumped so hard in her chest she was sure she'd have a heart attack any minute. *What was he going on about—and why was he so determined to arrest Kingi? Of course—he has probably worked out that he was the anonymous informer, but why does he want to capture him when it was Carlos who did the killing? It doesn't add up.*

'I think I should get out. I don't feel comfortable being driven by a bully.' Sandy went to open her door which was locked. 'I'll find my own way home—open my door!'

'Now, now. Don't overreact. The sun is starting to go down and I think you'll be a lot safer in the car with me than wandering around here by yourself. It'll be dark in an hour.'

Sandy felt like thumping him, but he was probably right. For the rest of the trip home, she said nothing and sat playing with her cell phone the whole journey while the scowl never left his face once. His cell phone kept ringing. Agitated, he switched it off—he didn't want to be found right now.

Sandy sat in the car thinking about how this could pan out. She would have to warn her friends about discovering Al's dark side. And what about Elly who is dating his colleague, Ben? What would he think of it all? They would have to keep their talk about the murder for another time and not discuss it on Lion Rock with Ben around—not until they were sure they could trust him. What a shemozzle this has turned out to be, she thought.

Her musings were interrupted by a gruff voice.

'Here you are—get out! And think hard about our little pep talk,' Al snarled, unlocking the door and driving off in a temper before her feet had hardly touched the ground.

Sandy's hands and knees shook so much she felt sick and in disbelief. She'd barely recovered from a horrific accident, witnessed a murder and now this. The knowledge of having an abusive, narcissistic cop in her neighbourhood was enough to amplify her Post Traumatic Stress Disorder.

She jumped out of her skin when her cell phone rang. 'It's Briar—I'm not going to be home till late—going to my parents' for dinner and just leaving work. Do you mind?'

Tonight of all nights, Sandy didn't feel like being alone—in fact, perhaps never after her nerve-wracking experience.

'Oh—I'll be alright—give my love to your folks,' she managed to get out with a quaver in her voice.

There was silence for a few seconds. 'Is everything okay with you, Sandy? It doesn't sound like it.'

'I've just had a bad experience today—but don't you worry, I'll be fine. We'll have a catch-up tomorrow after work.'

Briar was reluctant to stay away, hearing that her friend was not feeling so great, but Sandy had convinced her. Nevertheless, she had to warn the others about her upsetting clash with the detective.

She managed to scrape together a few leftovers for her evening meal and hurriedly rang Peter.

'It's Sandy—are you free this evening?'

'I was hoping you would ring. What do you think of the terrible news about poor old Jock? I wondered if you and Briar would like to meet up at Elly's tonight. Her brother is home and they would like to talk about it.'

A lump the size of a boulder hit the pit of Sandy's stomach and the remains of her meal catapulted up to her throat.

'What? What are you talking about—has Jock died?'

'It was on the 6 pm news tonight. He was found lying dead at the bottom of the cliff at Anawhata beach early this morning, and the police suspect foul play. I'm sorry to break the bad news. He was the key witness for Santos's murder and that just leaves you.'

'Unless Kingi was involved. They'll need him to testify,' Sandy said, bursting into tears trying to pull herself together so she could tell Peter her own daunting news.

'Oh, sorry Sandy. I didn't mean to shock you like this over the phone.'

'It's not just Jock—I have other startling news to tell you. I'd rather say it to your face though.'

'Can you come? I'll pick you up in half an hour and let the others know. Jock's death has shed new light on things.'

You can say that again—in more ways than one, Sandy was thinking.

'Sure—I'll be ready. I think I'd better phone Briar back quickly and ask her to come along. I don't think she has heard the news about Jock.'

'Don't worry about your car. I'll take you up there tomorrow and take a look at it. If I can't fix it, I'll get Mick, our local mechanic to tow it back to the beach.'

All she wanted to do was have a hot bath and snuggle up to Peter in front of the telly. But this was serious. Who would hurt such a gentle old man who was so harmless? Unless someone wanted him out of the way for some reason.

The fact that Jock was a key witness had been highly confidential, and unbeknown to Sandy only Peter knew his identity, as the witness statement he gave was anonymous.

Chapter Twenty-five

Sandy was surprised to see Elly's brother, Tim sitting in the lounge with her, as he usually wasn't around when she visited. Elly's hands shook while she handed around the cups of tea and cake, still upset about Jock's demise, as she liked him the day she and Peter had dropped in on him.

Briar had come straight from work after Sandy had phoned her, and Elly and Tim had filled her in on the news about Jock. She blushed as Tim showed his affection for her openly by squeezing in next to her on the couch.

'How are you, mate?' Tim said, as he stood and shook Peter's hand before almost sitting back on Briar's lap. 'Haven't seen you around for a while.'

'Been flat out for months,' said Peter. 'Plenty of work on. We must do some canyoning sometime soon.'

Sandy wanted to tell them to get to the point—the reason they were invited to the gathering, and Peter picked up on her restlessness.

'I guess you all want to talk about this latest death we've had here at the beach and whether the two are connected. Elly and I met Jock for the first time during Sandy's disappearance, but I know that you, Tim met Jock when he first moved here, when you were a young constable, Elly said.'

'Yep—that goes back a long way,' he replied.

Sandy was bursting to say something about the frightening incident she had with Al Crawford when Elly spoke.

'I noticed when Peter and I visited him to ask questions about Manuel Santos, there were quite a few houses along from Jock's with access to Anawhata Road,' said Elly.

Tim nodded at this sister. 'Yes, I know. Tell them the concern you had, Elly.'

'Oh, you mean what Ben said when he was complaining about Al. He said how he suddenly started snapping at him recently and seemed to have his own agenda without telling Ben about it. I suppose he was trying to tell me he appeared shifty.'

Sandy felt an electric jolt shoot through her when she said that.

'Oh, you must be kidding. This can't just be a coincidence. I've experienced something weird like that with him today!' Sandy couldn't restrain herself any longer. The tension was too much, and she burst into tears.

Peter stood up and walked over to her. 'Sandy—what's wrong—what happened?' He put his arm around her, his intuitive eyes searching her face.

'I didn't get a chance to tell you, but we have all been hoodwinked into believing that our Detective Inspector Crawford is a friend—but he's a scumbag!'

Everyone turned their gaze towards Sandy, all sitting with their mouths wide open at this unexpected outburst. Peter took hold of her hand. 'What is this, honey—what's he done?'

Sandy sobbed softly and between her snivelling and choking on her words, managed to tell it how it really was and that Al had threatened her.

Peter took an unused handkerchief out of his pocket. 'Here,' he said, tenderly wiping the tears from her cheeks and handing it to her to do the rest.

'What a chameleon,' blurted Elly. 'We need to report him to his superior or whatever he is called.'

Tim piped up all of a sudden. 'No—don't rush in like that. We have to find out what's behind all this and if there's corruption in the police force. We don't know who to trust.'

'I think we can trust Ben. He's only a Detective Sergeant, but he's also a Christian and I think he's genuine. He too has been concerned about Al lately, saying how he has been acting weird and secretive. If he asks questions about the Poderosa cartel case, Al gets defensive and doesn't let Ben get involved except with paperwork.'

'Look—there's something else you need to know. I thought it was just a coincidence at first, but now I'm not so sure.'

'What's wrong, Tim, tell us?' pleaded his sister.

'I don't want to throw in a red herring, but something strange happened to me today on the way back from Anawhata early this morning. After my run, around 7.30 am, as I drove along Anawhata Road, I saw Al's car tearing out of Jock's driveway. I don't think he recognised me, but I wondered why he was there so early in the morning.'

'What do you think he was doing?' asked Sandy.

'I've no idea—I just found it all a bit strange,' said Tim. 'It wasn't possible for him to be at the scene so early doing investigations when Jock's body wasn't discovered until after midday by a local swimmer. There was no one else around on that quiet weekday.'

Sandy squirmed. 'Ooh, that would have been while I was having lunch in Titirangi. To think all that was going on while I was eating.'

'How do you know that was Jock's driveway—have you been there before?' Briar asked Tim.

'Yes, when I was in the force. He had been harassed by a few youths who had been drinking at the beach and had stumbled upon his hut. There was also another time when the public complained when he went swimming in the nude. I got on well with him,' replied Tim.

'You never told me that!' said Elly.

'Police work was confidential. I couldn't discuss it at the time.'

'So what would Al be doing visiting Jock—and was it before or after his death?' asked Sandy.

Peter was beginning to wonder whether it was time for him to open up about the mistake he made—a mistake that may have cost Jock his life. He knew too well that his confession might threaten his relationship with Sandy, let alone the rest of his friends, but he couldn't hold on to it any longer as he had a strong conscience.

'There's something I need to tell you ... to do with Jock's death. I have to get something off my chest.'

Sandy glared at him, her eyes out on stalks. She clenched her teeth, waiting for him to drop the bombshell.

'I ... ah ... I hope it's not my fault that Jock's dead. I mistakenly identified him to Al as the anonymous witness to the slaying of Manuel Santos at Whites Beach. Jock saw the whole scene from beginning to end from the beach and could give a clear description of each of the men. He came to my house and dictated to me everything he saw and begged me to promise I wouldn't disclose his name and address if he would agree to be an anonymous witness.'

His friends sat gaping at him in silence— the grim expressions on their faces said it all.

'Now I'm afraid that for some reason, Al may have gone to him with the written witness statement to get him to change it—or worse.'

Tim looked at his sister and then at the others in the room who were lost for words.

'That's a felony—intimidating a witness if that's what he was doing. Are you suggesting that he may have something to do with Jock's death—for what reason, do you think?' asked Tim.

Peter held Sandy's hand. 'For the same reason, he threatened Sandy when he said she could end up washed up on the beach like Santos. Maybe he had just come from finishing Jock off and it was still fresh in his mind. He could be involved with this cartel in some way. I mean, they are not just into drugs, but also money laundering, illegal firearms and prostitution. Al may be profiteering from one of those things or more. There have been plenty of corrupt cops in New Zealand—several at the top.'

'Wow! That's one hefty synopsis. Do you honestly think he could be involved?' asked Elly

'I think it's on the cards. Maybe you should invite Ben over for dinner a few times and see if he can shed any light on it, without telling him what we know. He may help us solve it in the long run, but you have to make sure you can trust him first,' said Tim.

Elly screwed her nose up. 'Aw—isn't that using him kind of? I'd hate to frighten him off.'

'No, on the contrary. You want to see if he is relationship material, don't you? Well, what better way than to cook for him and get to know him. Take him off for a hike up by Jock's hut, or nearby. Maybe he'll open up. We need him to find the autopsy report and establish the time of death.'

'I suppose I could. I hope that horrible Al doesn't think I'm interfering and come after me—or him.'

'He doesn't see you as a threat,' said Tim.

'At least, not yet,' said Elly, shuddering. 'By the way—Ben said Al is dropping around to collect the things he left at his house tomorrow after work to take back to where he lives wherever that is. He had left some belongings there when he stayed at Ben's house while they were searching for Sandy and he was working half the night.'

'Mmm—I'd like to know where he lives. Perhaps one of us should follow him. What do you think?' asked Peter.

'It will be risky, but I could do that,' Tim replied. 'I think I'm the least threat to him at present. Elly—ask Ben to let you know what time Al is leaving his house. Tell Ben you want to visit as soon as Al has left. I'll hang around the beach in the car where he can't see me and once you phone me, I'll wait in the street nearby and follow him.'

'I suppose you could just be going into the village or out west. There's no harm in that even if he did recognise you, as there's only one road in and out so he can't suspect you,' said Peter.

'Let's do it! I'm all for it. Okay, Elly? Call Ben now and arrange to visit him tomorrow morning?' said Tim.

'Wait—there's something else,' said Elly. 'When Al first started working from the station here at the beach, one of my colleagues from the restaurant said she thought she knew where he lived. She was sure she saw him one night entering the gate of this huge mansion near her house in Fernhill, Titirangi. She said no one knows who owns it and various people stay there from time to time who aren't locals. It could be a private holiday home.'

'So what did Al do—was he with anyone that night?'

'No, she said the gate is remote controlled and there are Rottweiler dogs on the property that bark a lot.'

'Goodness, we must keep this under our hats for future reference. She may end up being a witness too,' said Tim. 'You'd better phone Ben and arrange to meet him at the house as we discussed.'

Elly agreed and went into another room to call him. Within a short time, she walked back into the lounge with a smile stretched across her face.

'Yep, it's all arranged.'

Peter smiled at Sandy, both enjoying seeing Elly's delight at having a reason to visit Ben.

'I don't think it's safe for Elly to follow Al home. I think I should do it,' said Tim. 'If he is implicated and I'm going to be a prosecuting attorney, I would need photos. Later the police will have to go with a court order to search the place.'

'Where do we go from here—I mean, so we get to know where Al lives—so what?' asked Briar.

'I'll wait around Glen Esk Road under a tree when Al is about to head out and follow him. You still need to make sure he has gone properly, Elly so when you get to Ben's place, text me.'

Tim turned to Briar. 'To answer your question—we have to dig up as much information about this man to try to piece together this macabre jigsaw and see if he is involved with corruption—and to what extent. He could be a ring leader for all we know,' said Tim.

Sandy shivered. 'Sounds dangerous to me. But we have to find out, for sure. There's something very dark going on with that man.'

Peter stood up ready to go out the door and beckoned Sandy to accompany him. 'I tell you all something for sure—that the key witness statement that Jock made, will no longer be used—Al will have taken care of that. You and Kingi are the only witnesses and Al knew that when he picked you up on the road. He had already got Jock out of the way and that's why he threatened you. I think that real soon we're going to have to take this to the top. What do you think, Tim? You're a prominent barrister in these parts. We'll have to be guided by you, as he'll be one step ahead of us.'

Tim stood up and paced back and forth. 'I guess I could do some work on how to deal with police corruption. Without naming anyone, I might be able to approach a few mates who are high up in the force to help, men I can trust.'

'I've got an idea. I could ask Ben to try to search any of Al's cell phones he might find at the station—proof of contacting Jock and any other dirt he can find on him,' said Elly.

Tim put an arm across his sister's shoulders protectively. 'But you have to make sure first that you can trust him completely. If not, it could blow this whole operation apart.'

Briar stayed back to have a cup of hot chocolate that Elly had offered. It also hadn't gone unnoticed that Tim couldn't stop looking at Briar the entire time during their meeting.

Peter, anxious to get away, drove Sandy home, but he had an agenda. He kissed her at the door after dropping her home and instead of saying goodbye he wanted to have some time with her on her own.

'Do you mind if I come in for hot a drink? I need to talk to you, as I'm not sure you are that safe in this house, especially when Briar is away at night. Can we talk about it?'

'You're welcome to come inside, Peter, but you're like Tim was with Briar, urging her to stay with her parents until all this blows over. He is sweet on her but can't commit.'

She took his hands and directed him to sit on the couch on the veranda.

'It's still quite mild, although autumn evenings will start to draw in soon. Look—I'm sure I'll be okay now that Al is moving away from the beach. Elly said she'll ask Ben to look after me. He walks past here each morning and goes for a walk along the beach at night keeping an eye on me ever since my rescue.'

'Maybe he has found a reason to do that— he may have his suspicions. If we could get him on our side, it would be a great help.' Peter wrapped his arms around her, kissed her warmly—a lingering kiss this time, and then pulled away, removing something from his pocket.

'Sandy, this is what I wanted to talk to you about. I feel I can't protect you the way things are, so if I were to become your husband, I could do a better job.'

Sandy sat aghast, ogling the small, blue velvet box he was about to open.

'Um ... what are you trying to say—I don't understand?'

She was oblivious to the fact that she was holding her breath and let it out with a loud noise.

'I am asking if you would let me have the honour of becoming my wife?' he said with a shaky voice as he took her hand and gently slipped a sapphire ring onto her finger.

Sandy was speechless. She had secretly hoped that Peter would one day have the courage to ask her to marry him.

Her eyes became like blue pools swimming in tears of joy. 'Yes, yes I will—I couldn't think of anything right now that could make my life complete.'

Immediately she was lost in romantic oblivion as they kissed more passionately than before. Within a short time, she stood up to make a hot chocolate for them both and they sat up until midnight sharing how long they had both known they harboured deep feelings for each other until Peter wrenched himself apart.

'I'd better go—sorry to disturb our bliss, but I have an early start tomorrow and it's after midnight. I'll phone you first thing in the morning to arrange to sort your car out.'

He kissed her again,' and stepped away. 'Night-night, my fiancée,' he said softly, as Sandy stood on the doorstep still lost in complete oblivion.

Chapter Twenty-six

Tim was so proud of his sleuthing in Fernhill, having captured explicit photographs of Al entering the mansion, exactly as his sister had described to him. Where would he get that kind of money? The property was fortified with two-metre high stone walls with a discreet row of stone thorns across the top—a lethal deterrent for any unaware intruder. Apart from the dogs, there were CCTV cameras everywhere and fortunately, Tim had the intelligence to camouflage his small camera in the bushes further away from the house. He had parked his car a little way up the road and wore a black hoody and raggedy jeans—a far cry from the sports suit he wore at his law practice.

When he arrived back at his office, he changed his clothes and jumped onto his computer, ready to do some research on this mansion by first googling the images. Funnily enough, there was nothing to be found—not even its last sale date. This, Tim, thought suspect in itself, as there must have been some history with a house like this. It was as though it never existed thanks to a cyber expert who had erased whatever information there was.

Tim, who was well known and respected in the Titirangi community as an attorney, discreetly made enquires in the community about the house. One of his colleagues had seen expensive cars, boats and motorbikes come and go from there on occasion. Apart from that—nothing.

🐾 🐾 🐾

Sandy took the mug of tea Briar offered her. 'He's finally popped the question! I thought he'd never ask. All this time he secretly loved me, he said, way before my accident. But I thought he was afraid of commitment.'

'Congratulations!' Briar wrapped her arms around her. 'Wow, that's an enigma—Pete committing. Well done, that's a first since I've known him.'

'He said when he saw me lying on the stretcher after I was rescued, he couldn't bear the thought of losing me.'

Sandy showed her the engagement ring.

'Goodness—that must have set him back a dollar or two. It's gorgeous—sapphires?'

'Yep, he's had a few major contracts that would have paid for that.'

'I'm so pleased for you, Sandy. It's about time you had a lift after all the mayhem that's been going on in your life.'

'Yeah, I guess it is. It has certainly lifted my spirits. He is so kind—he even managed to get my car going when it stalled up on Scenic Drive. Took him a while, but he fixed it.'

'He's a great bloke alright.'

'I hope you don't mind me asking, Briar, but how is Tim getting on with his investigation into this business with Dodgy Al? It has been a week now and I haven't heard anything—nor has Peter.'

'That's okay. It seems to be in hand—but didn't Ben tell you? They couldn't get Carlos for drug trafficking but found enough cocaine in the hull to convict him for possession. The police are determined to get him for smuggling but they need more evidence.'

'What a pity. I thought he would be behind bars by now,' said Briar, grimacing.

'They want me to do my remote witness video at the police headquarters out West this week, but they don't think that my witness statement alone would be enough to convict

Carlos with murder—but Jock's would have been,' said Sandy.

'Oh, that's a pain. There must be some way they can rake up enough dirt on him to put him away for a long time.'

'There's something else. But keep this to yourself, promise?' said Sandy.

'Sure—what's happened?'

Sandy was about to tell Briar she had received a letter from Kingi and then changed her mind. She had better save that privileged information for Peter. If the cat got out of the bag about Kingi's whereabouts, it could put his life at risk and that of his family.

'Never mind,' she said. 'I've got to get home. Ben Crosby wants to see me and make sure I'm ready to do the remote witness statement, and I have a few questions to ask him myself.'

🐈 🐈 🐈

'Do you want to stay and have a bit of dinner with me? It's just the lasagne I made last night,' Sandy asked, as Ben settled into an armchair.

'I'd love to—my favourite, but Elly's expecting me tonight as Tim's gone out for the evening.'

'I suppose you wish she was living on her own these days.'

'Not really—at present, I feel she is safer with her brother around, especially with you know who lurking around. Oh—sorry, Sandy. I didn't mean to ...'

'Don't worry, I'm fine. I understand. Funny you mention that as he hasn't been around for a while—in fact, not since Jock's death.'

'Yes, I know what you mean—he's hardly been down to the Piha station since working back at the headquarters. I've been working here in Piha mostly on my own. And I hear congratulations are in order—when is the big day?'

'That won't be for a while—we haven't been together that long. Can't rush these things you know.'

'Yes, I do know. I hope Elly and I get an invitation to the wedding,' he said, with a warm smile.

'Anyway—must get down to brass tacks. Here is the scenario that will be played out for your video interview. They may not stick to that per se, but it'll give you the main idea. You'll need to be at the headquarters at 2 pm on the dot.'

'Yep, I'll be ready.'

Ben got up and poured himself another glass of iced tea. 'There's something else I wanted to talk about—it's Al.'

Sandy's mouth dropped wide open. Was she hearing right?

'I need to know exactly what happened the day he picked you up in Titirangi Village and threatened you.'

Sandy was dumbfounded. It was the first time Ben had asked her that—and how did he know? She hadn't breathed a word to him.

'I ... how did you know about that?'

'Elly and Tim. Her brother was concerned after the evening you told them when you and Peter had visited. Elly finally told me yesterday, as she has been concerned about your welfare since then. I wish I had known earlier as I have real concerns, if not suspicions about my boss.'

Sandy told Ben the whole story from when she first thought a vehicle had been trailing her until he threatened her in his car.

'There is more. Did Tim tell you that he has suspicions about the mansion that Al lives in?'

'Yes, he did. But we can't get a search warrant just like that. We have to have more to go on than what we have, so far. Imagine my position if I got a warrant to search my superior's house, and it produced nothing in the way of evidence. He'd make sure I'd never work in the force again.'

'So how are we going to find out what he has hidden in that house? I don't believe he lives there all the time.'

'No, nor do I. He seems to have no fixed abode, at least right now. He has been known to stay with friends for short periods and uses work to justify it.'

'I did something which was rather risky the last week Al worked from Piha Station,' said Ben. 'He ducked out for a walk down to the coffee kiosk one morning and while he was gone, I searched the many pockets of his trench coat and discovered the blue cell phone you described—the one that you saw when he took you home that day. It's not the same phone he uses when he's working. That's a black one.'

'Oh, yes—the glove box was open, and he slammed it shut the minute I hopped into his car. He also had a gun.'

'I had a quick look at the phone log and he had cleared most of it, but he definitely had made a call at 5.45 am. The police had found Jock's cell phone on his dining room table and I'm having the log checked. If that call from Al is on there, it will be the first piece of real evidence I'll have in Jock's case.'

'What? You mean, you think Al could have killed Jock? Now you're creeping me out.'

'I don't know, but I'll have to find out why he met him at such an hour and has kept it quiet. That's something he should have told me that day. He went off stealthily, first to visit Jock and then to stalk you and later Jock was dead. I have to get on top of all his secretive behaviour and believe me—I will.'

'What about the gun—should he be carrying one?'

'That will be legitimate. He will have had it allocated to him to be used in a shootout with an armed offender.'

Ben picked up his briefcase and walked to the door. 'I'll pick you up around 1.15 pm to take you to the headquarters for the remote video interview.'

'If you don't mind, I'd appreciate that. Enjoy your evening with Elly tonight.'

'Will do, bye for now.'

Chapter Twenty-seven

Ben almost shot through the ceiling when Al walked into the office, as he hadn't expected him until the afternoon. Typical of him to do that—trying to catch him out.

'So—I see you haven't got very far with that pile of paperwork that was on your desk, the last time I looked. How are you getting on with Jock's case? Solved it yet?' he said, with a snide tone.

'I've had a few interruptions. People here think I'm the local police copper when there's no Constable around. I reckon they need one here during the day, not just at night. The locals come to tell me trivia like their dog has gone missing or someone is parking on their manicured lawn.'

Al continued to sneer at him.

'And no—I've got no further, apart from the autopsy report saying Jock received a hard blow to the head, either from the fall on the rocks or before he fell.' Ben turned his head away to avoid eye contact with Al. 'I can't understand why anyone would want to hurt such a nice old bloke like Jock.'

Al gave a nervous cough.

'Well keep working on it. I'm sure you'll sort it out. By the way, I may have to take you away from here soon and you'll have to work from the West Auckland Station. I've got a pile of cases there that need investigating, and they're short-staffed.'

'What? I can't do that, I live here and the commute is too great each day, especially on an early start. Surely they can manage without me.'

Al's glare shot daggers at him. 'You aren't needed here anymore. Get it?'

The sharp remark left Ben reeling. This cop certainly wasn't on his side and he let him know it. He shut his mouth and thought to himself he had his allies—he didn't need him and he also knew the man at the top, Al's superior, and so did his father who had been in the force. He wasn't going to let Al get to him.

'Is that all? I've got some important calls to make. I have to organise Sandy Barrett's remote video witness interview for tomorrow.'

'Oh yes, that too. It's not going to come to much—you do realise that, don't you?' said Al. 'She wasn't even able to describe the men's appearance in any way. It was all a blur.'

'Well, at this stage, it's the only witness statement we have now that poor Jock is dead.'

Out of the corner of his eye, Ben saw the smirk on Al's face.

'Okay, I'd better let you get on to solve this big case. By the way, they haven't been able to convict Carlos for smuggling yet—not enough evidence, apart from traces of cocaine in the hull of his yacht.'

'That's if Carlos is his name. It seems that was just the alias he used while in New Zealand. My research shows that his true identity is Pedro Silva, I've read from previous convictions.'

'Smart cookie, aren't you? Just the little scholar. Perhaps you should go and work for the CIB. Let's hope all your research pays off. Keep it up—I'll be off now,' he grumbled, picking up a pile of Ben's completed reports to take back to headquarters.

Chapter Twenty-eight

Peter took the day off to spend with Sandy to give her respite from Piha and the doom and gloom of two ongoing murder enquiries in the community.

'All packed, are we?' he asked.

'Yep, I've got enough food for both of us and pump bottles with cranberry juice. Have you got all the kayaking gear sorted yet?'

'Sure have. Just need a hand to get them on the roof rack.'

Sandy traipsed after him out to his Ute parked in her driveway. Although they both had lightweight Barracuda kayaks, Sandy loathed the job of having to help Peter get the two of them onto the roof rack. She was shorter than him which made it more difficult, and she almost needed a small step to climb on.

Relieved they had successfully secured the kayaks, she climbed into the Ute, desperate to get away from it all for the day.

As they drove up the hill from Piha, they passed Al on his way to the police station again. He seemed to be snooping around more than usual, Sandy thought. *Trying to keep a closer eye on Ben, I'll bet.*

The beach at Laingholm was quiet and the water perfectly calm. Sandy remembered going there numerous times during her childhood.

As they unloaded the kayaks, Sandy recalled that Kingi had lived in Laingholm before he went into rehab. *Poor Kingi—so sad having to give all this up to flee to the South Island.*

Peter interrupted her thoughts. 'We'll just put them in over there off the beach. We don't need the boat ramp. Perhaps we could go for a paddle and then have lunch under the trees.'

Sandy was still in deep thought as they paddled across the bay and back. Each time she looked up at the treeline above the Laingholm dairy, she was reminded of Kingi who had owned a house near the shop. *What has become of it—is it sold?*

'Take a look at the pair of kingfishers on that branch. I don't think I've ever been this close to them. Can you hold my kayak for a minute?'

Peter took a few snapshots of the two lovebirds before they turned around and paddled back to Laingholm close to the shoreline.

Sandy had carried the load of knowing that Kingi was in the country and had gone south to work things out with his partner. But this morning, she had another burden to carry that she knew she could not deal with alone—an unsigned letter from Kingi who must have got a friend to post it in Auckland. He wrote to let her know he was safe and living happily with his partner and child in the mountains down south. But this time he warned her that she was in danger now that she was a witness to Manuel's murder. But the caution wasn't about Carlos—it was Al Crawford. For the first time, Kingi disclosed that Al was the cartel ring leader and not Carlos who was his hitman and did his dirty work for him when it came to thuggeries such as assault and murder. Al had masterminded the cocaine smuggling—not only in New Zealand but also in Australia, and he would make sure he had no witnesses. He was the drug baron.

They pulled their kayaks up on the grass and Peter brought a blanket out of the Ute to sit on while Sandy unpacked their lunch from the chilly bin. She knew that she was not going to be able to keep this latest news about Kingi to herself and especially the information about Al as she felt powerless and unable to know how to free herself from the threat of this man.

Look—there's something else we have to deal with—something that is going to blow your mind.'

'Oh dear—just when I thought we were going to have a lovely, relaxing afternoon together. Okay—spit it out.'

'Well, at least you're sitting down to get the bad news,' she said, handing him a drink bottle and muesli bar.

'I haven't entirely been upfront with you—I've been keeping something from you.'

Peter munched away on his sandwiches fixated on her every word as she told about Kingi's visit to her house that night when he had confessed everything.

'Oh my goodness—jumping Jehoshaphat! I knew he was up to no good—now I understand why he had to get rid of Jock. But why didn't you come to me with all this?'

'I was afraid you would go to the police, and I promised him I wouldn't tell anyone. He didn't want Carlos to know he had snitched on him.'

'So much for our relaxing day away for it all.' Peter gave her a half-smile, his expression full of disappointment.

'I'm sorry, honey. I didn't mean to bring it up today, but now that we think Al is suspect and may have removed Jock as a key witness, he will be desperate to track Kingi down. I don't know what to do—who to turn to,' she said, as her bottom lip quivered, her eyes welling up with tears. 'I don't know who I can trust anymore.'

Peter pulled her close and kissed her forehead, stroking her hair. 'It's going to be okay—don't worry. I think Ben is on our side and his father used to be high up in the force. I think we have to talk to him. He already has his doubts about Al and so does Tim and he's a lawyer.'

Sandy suddenly lost her appetite, wrapping her sandwiches up and placing them back into the chilly bin.

'I don't think I'm ever going to be able to relax again until Jock's murderer and the ring leaders of that cartel are behind bars.'

'I know—I have been feeling the same way. Let's load the kayaks and head back to the beach. We have to get this sorted,' said Peter, beginning to pack up the food.

'Kingi said he would do a remote video interview but will remain anonymous. He asked that I keep his phone number somewhere safe and destroy the letter he sent me,' said Sandy as she walked towards the Ute with the chilly bin.

'Al mustn't discover his whereabouts. He's not prepared to provide evidence unless he has been arrested and we'll have to go above him and get an investigation started somehow.'

'Let's get back to the beach and see if Ben can meet with us tonight. I'll ask Tim to be there too,' said Peter, taking one end of a kayak while Sandy lifted the other onto the roof rack.

After they strapped both kayaks on the rack, they wasted no time heading back to Piha.

'I suppose I ruined the day by bringing all this up,' said Sandy, lowering her gaze.

'Don't say that. I'm glad you could trust me enough to tell me—you had to tell someone. We need to be strong now, as we are involved with police corruption at top-level, but we know Ben is on our side and also his father.'

After they had offloaded the kayaks, Peter drove to the police station and found Ben's vehicle was still there, but Al had already gone. Sandy sat in the car while Peter arranged with Ben to meet at his house at seven. Later he phoned Tim, who agreed to be there with Elly, but she was visiting her parents. Peter guessed she felt safe away from the beach.

When they arrived at Ben's house, he had good news which he quickly offloaded. 'I have an ally in my father's friend, Detective Superintendent Max Truman from the Anti-Corruption Unit who has pulled strings to keep me at Piha Station. They have suspected Al Crawford for years, waiting for him to put a foot wrong, but up until now have had no incriminating evidence. Al is slippery and always seems to be one step ahead of them. Max has given his word he will set the wheels in motion for an underground investigation, and said that I can submit whatever evidence I can, aided by Tim, as Prosecutor.'

'That's good to hear, as I don't want you to leave here either. But this will only aggravate Al even more,' said Sandy. 'So where do we go from here? It all sounds so complicated and I'm afraid he will find out what we're up to.'

'Not if I can help it,' said Ben. 'We have to do everything undercover. Best you all leave the sleuthing to me as I can keep my finger on the pulse, but you can report to me anything— absolutely anything you may find pertinent to the case. But please—stay away from Al, he is a dangerous man.'

Sandy shuddered, wrapping her arms around herself.

'We can work together on this, Ben,' said Tim. 'I've already put together a case with the bits of evidence we have gathered so far. But the one thing we need which will be difficult to obtain is a witness statement from Kingi Walker.'

Sandy squirmed. *How was she going to protect him now? And what about his partner and that baby of his?*

'Sandy, we have submitted your remote video witness interview to the Australian court, but it isn't enough to convict Carlos—or should I say, Pedro Silva, seeing that is his real name.

Carlos doesn't exist. It's a pity we no longer have Jock to testify who could give conclusive evidence.'

'But you have my evidence. He spoke to me and I gave a written statement which I handed to Al. Do you still have it?' said Peter, his brow furrowing.

'No, he kept it. I guess he was trying to get Jock to change it,' said Ben, wiping his temples. 'It went missing that day that Jock was killed.'

'I kept a copy which I will swear is the statement Jock gave me. I'll get it to you and will stand by it,' said Peter.

Ben's face brightened. 'That is the best evidence we have to nail this Pedro guy for murder. But we need to get Kingi to help us to testify against Al and his associates. I can understand he would be afraid of reprisals with a partner and baby.'

Sandy looked solemn, biting her nails. The stress was beginning to show in her face too, and Peter couldn't help focusing on the dark circles around her eyes.

'You said you have Kingi's phone number,' said Ben. 'How about phoning him on a disposable phone like he uses, and plead with him to do a remote video witness interview testifying against Al. We will safeguard that phone after your call for the court hearing. If he agrees, I will let Max from the Anti-Corruption Unit know, as I'll keep in touch with him throughout this case. But you must all watch your backs. Al mustn't know anything about this. The Unit won't arrest him until they have enough evidence to hold him on remand without bail.'

'Wow—that would be so good if he was locked up. I feel unsafe with him lurking around,' said Sandy.

'I'm going to organise your witness protection through the Anti-Corruption Unit instead of the local police force and have security cameras around your whole house, instead of just at the front and back. That means no one will come near your place without being caught on video.'

'I'd much rather see her move in with Elly and Tim or go and stay with her parents,' said Peter, squeezing Sandy's hand.

'No, it's best she stays in her house. That way we will be able to catch Al if he is stalking you. I'll get our tech guys to set up the panic buttons so they send an alert to my phone as well as to the West Auckland station. They'll take too long to get here, but I can be at your house in two minutes. It will also resound so loudly through that speaker on your roof that people will hear it for miles. He's not going to commit murder here on the beachfront with so many people around.'

'Gee, thanks,' said Sandy grimacing.

If only we were married, she would be safe with me, Peter was thinking.

🐾 🐾 🐾

After finishing editing an article for the women's magazine next day, Sandy went for a run along Piha Beach as far as Barnett Hall with Sleuth beside her for the first time since her accident. She was completely healed but resented the fact that she had to bear the mental stress caused by the double murder that had taken place in what had once been a quiet, peaceful community. Her faith had given her the strength to cope, but anyone in this situation would find it unnerving, no matter how strong their faith.

Sleuth, oblivious to the turmoil thrashing inside her, was in his element chasing the seagulls and jumping into the shallow surf. Sandy was quickly reminded that without this canine saviour's devotion to her, she would be dead. He was her guardian angel.

At Barnett Hall, she put Sleuth on the lead and ran further up the beach to North Piha. When they arrived at the bottom of the steps that led to the lookout, the dog pulled away trying to turn around to go back—quite the contrary to how he had been when Peter took him for walks when she was missing.

Sandy hesitated, while Sleuth tugged on his lead. She glanced up at the track and felt a pain in her head as a haunting memory of recent events bombarded her brain.

'Come on, boy, I understand—I felt it too. Let's get out of here.'

She tightened her grip on his lead and took off back home, running along the sand with Sleuth running faster than ever beside her until they arrived back at Barnett Hall. She noticed Ben's car was still there but Al's had gone. She leaned on the window and waved to him and he beckoned her to wait.

He hurried around the side of the building and pulled out his phone.

'See this, you're on candid camera,' he chuckled.

Sandy looked at the video as clear as day of her walking around to the garden shed to get Sleuth's lead and to the other side of the house calling the dog. She watched as she saw herself talking away to Sleuth and taking him off down the beach.

'There you are—completely Al proof,' he said, bright-eyed. 'All set now. Let's hope we get the rest of the proof we need of him tampering with witnesses.'

'I'd rather he tampered with someone else though. Still, I have Sleuth at my side in the house. He won't want to mess with him or he'll rip him apart.'

'Okay, I must get on—got some deadlines to meet before I go home.'

'Thanks again, Ben. I appreciate your concern. I couldn't get hold of Kingi, his phone must have been off but I'll keep trying and let you know what he says.'

Chapter Thirty

It felt uncanny knowing there was a camera on her the minute she set foot on her property. She'd realised she'd forgotten to warn Briar about the new cameras as she walked around the side of the house and placed Sleuth's lead in the garden shed before refilling his water bowl. As she walked back to the front of the house, she inhaled the nostalgic aroma of Briar's tasty Shepherd's Pie, a welcoming surprise.

'Hi there—nice of you to cook tonight. I thought you would still be at your parents, waiting for all the drama to die down.'

Briar carried the hot casserole dish to the table while Sandy washed her hands at the sink.

'I've got some of that apple cider you like. I think it's called Monteith's Lightly Crushed. That will go well with it,' said Sandy, removing a bottle from the fridge.

They sat down to the meal and caught up.

'I'm sorry, Briar I forgot to tell you that the techs have installed two extra hidden cameras around the house today. There's a new one above the garden shed and the other is in the Puriri tree focused on the window at the side of the house.'

'Oh no, you mean they are watching us while we're eating. What if I had been walking around the house in my underwear?'

'No, of course not. The cameras are only on the outside of the house.'

'Thank goodness for that,' she giggled.

'It's for evidence of unwanted guests. And just to let you know—Al has been cautioned by his boss that he to keep his distance from me. Ben is the only one allowed to come to the house, and if Al needs to question me, he has to do it at the station with Ben or another accompanying police officer. Al only knows about the cameras at the front and back doors—not the ones at both sides of our property.'

'Wow—that's radical. It's about time someone put him in his place. I'm sick of all this talk about him—let's eat.'

Sandy was so relieved to have Briar home again. She knew her folks were worried that she chose to stay in her own home, but she was determined not to let Al or his accomplices drive her away and had reassured them that she was under police protection.

'Thanks for the lovely dinner—just what I needed. Let's go sit in the lounge,' said Sandy, stretching her arms in the air.

'Wait—there's dessert. I made a yummy crumble, but this time with blueberries. There's cream to go with it.'

'Ooh, sounds delicious. I'll have it a little later if that's okay.'

'Sure—I need to wait a while too. Plenty of time,' said Briar, closing the fridge.

They spent the rest of the evening watching a movie on TV, and before they turned in, they dished up dessert.

'What are you doing tomorrow?' asked Briar.

Sandy looked at her watch to check the date.

'I've got an acrylic painting I want to get finished for a tourist who had attended my exhibition at the Coastal Art Festival at Christmas. She wants to take it back to England with her.'

'That's awesome—you did well at that festival. Are you going to be involved in the Wild West Coast Art Tour coming up soon?'

'Yep—but my studio looks a shambles and I need to clean up the gallery too. I'll have to get on to it and work hard to turn up enough paintings to make it worth my while.'

'Maybe you should stick up a painting of Al on the wall with his hands around Jock's throat. That'll give him something to think about,' said Briar, chuckling to herself.

'I hope you're joking—he'll kill me if I do that. He wants my guts for garters now, anyway. I wouldn't need to provoke him as well—unless I paint the boat with Manuel, Pedro and Kingi pulling into Whites Beach.'

The two women continued their banter as they finished off their dessert.

'I'm going out with Tim tomorrow evening. He's taking me into the city to a new restaurant that has opened up on the waterfront.'

'Oh really? That sounds posh. How are you two getting on—anything serious?' asked Sandy.

'Well, I suppose we've moved to another stage from polite niceties over the phone to kissing and cuddling. That's progress, I guess. We aren't in a rush, so nothing too serious yet.'

'Neither are we—haven't got a wedding date yet. I need to be sure I'm in for no surprises. I mean—take a look at Al, the proverbial charmer and complete gentleman at first—a wolf in sheep's clothing. I'm not saying Peter is anything like him, but I will not throw caution to the wind.'

'You're wise not rushing ahead until all this police stuff blows over. You want to be able to focus on each other instead of all the aggro so you can get to know each other.'

'I might turn in now and take a book to bed. If I don't see you in the morning, have a lovely time with Tim.'

'Sure will—g'night.'

🐈 🐈 🐈

Three days later, Briar set off to work early in the morning and although Sandy had been woken early, she missed her going out the door. She'd been up since the crack of dawn to work on the masterpiece that she promised the tourist who would drop around to collect it that evening. The large painting of Piha with Lion Rock was her most popular work, and she'd sold many.

As she began adding her contrasting colours to the rock, she remembered how life was before her accident when she, Peter and Elly used to meet each morning before work to share and meditate at the summit. Life seemed so innocent and simple then.

As she carefully selected all the colours she needed and placed them on her palette, joy filled her heart at the opportunity to lose herself mentally during her painting—a satisfying release she found from the crazy world that surrounded her.

The morning sun streamed through the door of her studio shedding its rays on her shoulders. It was a perfect autumn day, inviting her to go for a surf, but she had to focus and get this painting finished. It would pay enough to supplement her rent for the next few months, although her father charged her and Briar hardly anything.

Something brushed her shoulder causing her to drop her palette and her heart to race. Blinded by the sun's rays, she turned to see the silhouette of a man towering above her. She took a few steps back and realised it was Al dressed in a different coat and hat that she didn't recognise.

'What are you doing here?' she shouted, pushing his hand away. 'You aren't allowed to visit—get out!' She tried not to look up at the camera that would have him in its sight, on the garden shed next to the studio.

Her first instinct was to run inside and hit the panic button, but he grabbed her arm. Sleuth was still inside the house and barked frantically and then stood snarling at the window.

'Whoa! Don't panic—be sensible about this, I'm not doing you any harm. I need to clarify something with you.'

'I have no cause to talk to you—Ben is handling my file. If you don't leave ... I'll ...' She pulled her phone from her smock pocket pressing the record button which was highlighted in red.

'Call the police will you?' he mocked with an evil glare in his eyes. 'I don't think so. Just remember what I told you when we went for that wee ride in my car. Perhaps you need reminding,' he said, as Sandy slipped the phone back inside her smock.

She was tempted to bring Sleuth outside who would attack him, but she couldn't tell if Al was armed, and he would certainly shoot the dog dead.

'All you have to do is give me Kingi's contact details. I know he is a key witness in that death and if he testifies, we can put Pedro away for life.'

Sandy was confused. She stopped to get her head around it. She knew that Kingi had phoned the police contact centre as an informer and told about the assault on Santos and that he and Sandy have history. If what Kingi says is true about Al being involved with the cartel as Ben suspects, then Al will want to stop Kingi from testifying against him. That's why he is so desperate to track him down. Perhaps he plans to destroy him too.

'No way. Why would I do that and let you take out another innocent man?'

'Him innocent—you must be dreaming, love.'

'I don't care—just get off my property or I'll call Ben,' she snapped, as she reached into the pocket of her artist's smock and kept her hand on it.

'Okay, okay—I'm going. But you'll regret tangling with me—you mark my words.'

He rushed off out the gate onto Marine Parade in a rage, scampering along the sidewalk to where he parked his car. He must have approached her property with stealth, Sandy thought, as he would usually park outside her gate. But this time, his presence had been noted.

She went inside the house and, still shaking, let Sleuth out into the backyard. He ran around scaling the fence line of the property and then came back inside almost licking Sandy to death.

'It's okay, boy. He didn't hurt me, but if he comes near me again, I'll let you take a piece out of him,' she said, stroking his head, trying to hold back her tears as the nervous tension began to show.

After pouring a coffee, she took her cell phone out of her pocket and played back the recording she had made of Al's whole conversation with her. She'd got him. Excitedly she phoned Ben.

'He's been around again. Can you check the video and show it to me? I managed to record his conversation.'

'I'll check it and be around soon. That's great news.'

Sandy sat at the dining table trying to settle her nerves after yet another disturbing incident with Al. Now she was more resolute than ever in making sure this monster would get his dues. She must get hold of Kingi.

In no time at all, Ben had arrived with the video clips to show her.

'It's perfect, said Ben as he finished running the footage. That, together with what you have on your phone is sufficient to run him in. I'm going to take this to Max to get the wheels in motion for his arrest. I'll phone him after I leave here. Do you mind if I borrow your phone for the afternoon? I can leave you with this disposable one for emergencies. Here—my telephone number is on this card,' he said, handing her his business card. 'You'll have your phone back by the end of the day.'

Ben didn't even stop for a coffee. He shot out the door full of gusto and took off in his vehicle before Sandy could say much more.

Her motivation to finish the painting had left her. She went to her address book and looked up the phone number of the tourist and asked her to collect the finished product in the morning. There was no way she could find the inspiration to complete it that afternoon. But there was a flicker of hope stirring in her soul that for the first time in months, she felt there was a real breakthrough and they had some concrete evidence to produce. Not only at the trial of Pedro Silva's but also at that of Detective Inspector Al Crawford.

Chapter Thirty-one

'Kingi, is that you? It's Sandy,' she said, trying to adjust to the disposable phone that Ben told her to use for this call. 'I need your help.'

Sandy talked at length about how she and her friends had the backing of Ben and his father's friend, Max and the Anti-Corruption Unit to put Al behind bars and needed him to do a remote video interview under the Witness Protection Scheme, just as she had done for the Pedro Silva trial.

'I'm not doing anything unless I have Max Truman's word that I will not be arrested and have no criminal charges brought against me. I want your word from him that this will happen. He can phone me on a different number—a disposable phone which I'll destroy after the call. If he does that, I'll give him names and addresses of Pedro Silva and his associates. They used a house that Al stays in at Fernhill to store illegal goods such as firearms, drugs and laundered money. Ask Max to get a warrant to have the place searched. It's a minefield.'

Sandy went quiet. There was so much for her to take in and she had scribbled the conversation down on a jotter pad as fast as she could, ready to take to Ben, including the address of the infamous house he mentioned.

'Get back to me and tell me if Max agrees to do this and then I'll arrange a time to ring me. I need that reassurance from him that I will not be arrested. That has to be the deal. They will not get to know my whereabouts.'

'I'll do it—I'll sort it and get back to you. Oh, Kingi thanks so much—you've no idea how much grief you are saving me and the rest of this community by helping put Al behind bars.'

'Just get back to me as soon as you can. I want this whole thing to be over too so I can move on with my life. I've already started afresh, but this is hanging over me.'

'I will, I promise. God Bless.'

🐈 🐈 🐈

One week later

Ben had convinced Max to agree that if Kingi supplied him with the names, whereabouts and activities of the cartel leaders

247

via an anonymous video interview, that he would not be arrested. With Kingi's video testimony and a list of names and places he gave them, they had sufficient evidence for a case against Al Crawford.

Max sat in Al's chair in the office at the police station at Piha, contemplating how to go about arresting Al Crawford.

After handing him a mug of coffee, Ben set the criminal evidence documents before him, which he had gathered.

'I think we have enough to prosecute—but let's wait until we get the results of the house search tomorrow,' said Max. 'He has no idea we're sending our people in. They are going with a search warrant at dawn.'

'Well, I for one would like to be a fly on the wall and see the look on his arrogant face for once,' said Ben, with a set jaw.

'I don't think you'd better be there—leave it to me. We'll arrest him on the spot if there is any of the stuff Kingi said would be there, and I know how hard it would be to arrest a colleague you've been working with.'

'Sure, I get your drift. I prefer to stay here and let you do it. What's the progress with the Pedro case? Any convictions yet?'

'He has had a preliminary hearing over the drug trafficking charge, but they are waiting for the outcome of these investigations as it will lead to a joint trial with Al and multiple defendants in New Zealand.'

Max picked up the dossier. 'I've got to get on. I'll let you know the results of the search tomorrow. I've posted Kingi a written statement signed by me that he will not be arrested for supplying us with the video witness interview. I'll be in touch,' said Max as he walked towards the door.

'Thanks, Max. I wouldn't have been able to pull this off without you. Thanks again for trusting me.'

Max drove off, leaving Ben overwhelmed by all that had taken place. He couldn't believe the progress they had made—that Al Crawford's day of reckoning was imminent. He despised the fact that he had put his trust in him from the outset and he turned out to be a complete traitor, not to mention the abuse of Peter's fiancée. But what put a chill down his spine even more so, was the fact that the mobster infiltrated Ben's peaceful community of Piha Beach, gaining the trust of innocent residents to build his drug empire.

He'd had enough for the day. He rubbed his strained eyes and yawned. Every part of him seemed to ache as though he had run a marathon—but he had in a way, he thought. A mental marathon—a battle of the wits. But he believed he had God on his side—a strong and mighty tower. He got up and switched off the lights, set the alarms and locked up. This evening he had promised to shout Elly a takeaway meal at his house and hoped she wouldn't say no to a good movie on TV afterwards. That would be all he could manage in one day.

Chapter Thirty-two

Sandy arrived on Peter's doorstep just as he took the roast out of the oven.

'Let yourself in—it's not locked,' he called from the kitchen. Sandy found him in a comical apron, holding padded gloves and a roasting dish.

'Sit yourself down in the dining room—I'm about to dish up.'

Sandy was surprised to see the table set to the standard of a posh hotel, with a starched white tablecloth and the finest stainless steel cutlery. He had even added a small white vase with little rosebuds and crystal wine glasses. In the background played her favourite music—Burt Bacharach.

When he sat down at the table after carving the chicken she asked, 'What's all this in aid of—you aren't going to propose to me again, are you?'

He laughed and passed her the roast vegetables. 'We have something to celebrate.' He stood up and took a bottle from the fridge. 'Bubbly for the occasion too, but next it will be champagne.'

'What's going on—I don't understand?'

'Ben has been trying to get hold of you. He dropped in earlier to give me all the news. He asked if you could phone him tonight or in the morning.'

'Oh, I've been working all day and forgot to turn my cell phone on. What's up?'

'It's Al—the Anti-Corruption Unit have arrested him and he is in custody,' he said, pouring the Chardonnay into the glasses.

'What happened?'

'They did a blitz on the house he was staying in—you know—the one that Tim followed him to and discovered a minefield. They found illegal firearms, laundered money, more drugs and possible stolen goods. Apparently, that was just one house he frequents as do his henchmen, who all utilise it as a cover.'

'Unbelievable,' she said, wiping gravy from her lips with a paper napkin.

'They are holding him on remand without bail. Pedro is being transported over here tomorrow to be tried in New Zealand instead. It's going to be a joint trial using Kingi's testimony and yours.'

'But that means after they serve their sentences and are released, they could stalk me.'

'No way. Ben said that it looks like Al was the drug baron, not Pedro who was just one of his pawns and a hitman. Al was the one with all the power who called the shots. Because of their history, they are both likely to get double or triple life sentences. If Pedro is ever released, he will be deported back to Brazil.'

'Wow—it certainly is grounds for celebration. I just can't believe it.'

'Give Ben a call tomorrow—he can enlighten you more.'

The two of them relaxed and laughed for the first time in months. They sat at the table and swapped banter for a short time and then snuggled up on the couch.

'Briar and I are going to a sportswear sale tomorrow morning on her half day.'

'Oh, I see—shopping for more of those bright red sports bras, are you,' he asked, winking and nudging her in the ribs.

'What? Oh, no, I forgot about that. I clean forgot that you must have seen it when Sleuth went to fetch you that day.'

They both laughed and made light of it.

'I think we should start thinking about setting a date for our wedding soon—what do you think?' Peter asked, tentatively.

'That sounds like a great idea, but not until those evil men are locked up for good.'

For the rest of the evening, Sandy struggled to stay awake. She gently pulled away from Peter's arms and picked up her handbag. 'I'll have to get off now—can barely keep my eyes open.' She bent over and kissed him, sweetly.

'Wait—I'll see you out to your car.'

🐈 🐈 🐈

The joint trial took weeks and although Sandy wasn't required to be at the court and had provided the remote witness video interview just as Kingi had done, she was still part of the trial. The lawyers and police teams involved her in many discussions.

By the end of the month, the jury had declared Al guilty of one account of the murder of Jock, an accessory to the murder of Manuel Santos and another murder of a witness in Sydney. He was sentenced to back to back double life sentences and Pedro was given the same for the murder of Santos and previous killings. They both had extra jail time added to their sentences for the illegal firearms, money laundering and theft. The handgun that Sandy had seen had not been allocated by the Police Department. It was an illegal weapon.

Sandy and Peter sat with Ben and Elly on Lion Rock watching the sun popping up behind the sea's horizon. 'What will become of Kingi,' Sandy asked Ben after they had given thanks to God for helping them solve the crimes.

'I guess he'll get on with his life with his partner and child and put it all behind him in incognito,' he said, placing his arm around Elly who snuggled into his side, pulling her closer. 'He is changing his name by deed poll under the Witness Protection Scheme and then he's getting married. I guess he has finally worked out what is more important in life—that love and people matter more than money and power,' he said, winking at Elly.

'I hear it's thanks to you, Sandy and the help and encouragement you gave him in rehab that he decided to turn his life around. That's why he couldn't let anyone hurt you and he came clean.'

'I guess so,' said Sandy humbly.

'It goes to show that something really good came from your terrible accident, as well as showing me how important you are to me,' said Peter, squeezing her hand tight.

'Yeah,' she nodded, 'What was intended for evil, God used for good, to save many lives— I guess that's what you're trying to say?'

They all went quiet, gazing at the glorious changing colours of the sunrise—the sky a majestic bright orange and red, and this time, a rainbow with a show of promise and hope for their future.

🦌 🦌 🦌 THE END 🦌 🦌 🦌

Author – Patricia Snelling

Patricia, known as Trish, grew up in a small town in New Zealand. From the age of five, she rode horses which her family owned and trained, often winning prizes in the local horse shows. During her early life, her parents lived off the land, initially share-milking and later as horticulturalists.

After completing her nursing studies and qualifying as a Registered Nurse, Patricia spent six years abroad, living in Australia and Europe doing a variety of jobs between her nursing roles and returned to Auckland to start a family. After a forty-year nursing career, Patricia retired and now writes inspirational Cosy Mysteries, Adventure and Romantic Suspense set in beautiful New Zealand

PLEASE VISIT ME ON MY WEBSITE

patriciasnelling.com